Calum has been living with the badgers for months now, but he's still an outsider, and it's entirely his fault. His past influences how he behaves, and it's easier to push everyone away than to allow them in and risk losing them.

Duane just left the military and is looking for a new direction. When he applies for a job as a guard in the forest where the shifters live, he doesn't expect much, and certainly not to stumble on two guys having words in the grocery store. He steps in, acts as a fake boyfriend, and starts falling for Calum.

But Calum's fears run deep, and Duane doesn't know if he belongs in the forest. If those were the only problems, Duane wouldn't doubt they could make it work, but someone in the forest is plotting something, and they might have involved humans.

The forest is in danger, as is Calum's heart. Will Calum be able to see beyond his fears? Can Duane convince him they can have their own happily-ever-after?

Clear Skies
Copyright © 2022 Catherine Lievens
ISBN: 978-1-4874-3708-4
Cover art by Angela Waters

Published by eXtasy Books Inc

Look for us online at:
www.eXtasybooks.com

CLEAR SKIES
ALLEGHENY SHIFTERS 11

BY

CATHERINE LIEVENS

CHAPTER ONE

Julian started getting up from the couch, but Calum shot to his feet and glared at him. Julian looked amused, but thankfully, he sat back down and pressed his hands against his swollen stomach.

"I was just getting some water," he said.

"I'll get it for you. I already told you and Kaspar that I'll take care of you, and it's why I'm here after all."

Julian frowned. "You're not here to help us. You're here because you're our family."

Calum's heart fluttered. How was Julian so much older than him yet so adorable? He shouldn't be, but Calum suspected that his pregnancy had a lot to do with it. Not everything, though. Julian was a good man, and Calum loved him.

"He's right," Kaspar said from next to Julian. "Even if you didn't lift one finger in the house, we'd still want you here."

Calum snorted. "If I didn't lift a finger, I wouldn't want me here." Because no matter what they said, Calum was here first and foremost to help them with their pregnancies.

He'd been stunned when he'd found out that both Julian and Kaspar were pregnant, although he supposed he'd been nowhere near as stunned as they had. Julian had thought he couldn't have any more children, and when they'd decided to start a family, they'd thought Kaspar was the only one who could get pregnant.

They'd been wrong.

Now, both of them were heavily pregnant and about to pop. Julian's due date was first, but Kaspar wouldn't be far behind, and once they both gave birth, the house would be a mess of babies and tired fathers.

Calum couldn't wait.

He wasn't an idiot. He realized that most people he'd lived with at the Bishop house didn't like him. It was his fault because he'd isolated himself and had convinced himself he didn't need anyone to survive, not even the badgers. But he'd been wrong.

He was glad Julian and Kaspar had seen through his shell and decided to give him a chance. That was why he was here. He'd offered to help them with the babies when they came, and they'd accepted that offer. They'd given him a chance he'd never thought he'd have, and he'd forever be grateful for that.

But that wasn't the only thing he was grateful for. They'd given him an out, and he hadn't had to return to the bats. He'd been terrified he'd be forced to, but he should have known better. Even without Julian and Kaspar, Thomas wouldn't have forced him to go anywhere, even though Calum hadn't told him why he decided to leave his home permanently.

He headed to the kitchen, filled a glass of water for Julian, then paused. "Kaspar?" he called out.

"Yes?"

"Do you need anything, since I'm here?"

There was a moment of silence, and Calum heard Julian chuckle. Then, Kaspar answered, "A glass of water would be good."

Calum would have brought him one even if he hadn't wanted it. The dads needed to stay hydrated, and Calum was on it.

He carried the glasses back to the living room and handed them over. He sat back in the armchair, gesturing at Julian to put his feet up on his lap.

"You don't have to do this," Julian said, but he was already lifting his feet.

Even though he was barefoot, they were swollen, and Calum started rubbing them. He'd have been horrified at the thought of doing something like this for anyone else, but Kaspar and Julian had become his family. He'd never been as close to anyone as he was to them, not even his parents.

Julian moaned a little, and Calum didn't miss the way Kaspar peered at him. He swallowed and looked away, feeling like he was intruding on a situation he shouldn't be. Julian and Kaspar were very much in love, and in any other circumstance, Calum wouldn't be living with them. If just Kaspar had been pregnant, Julian would be rubbing his feet right now, and it would probably end in sex on the couch. Instead, both of them were so big they could barely get back to their feet once they sat on the couch, so there would be no hanky-panky today, especially not with Calum right there. He had no idea if the two men still had sex, and he wasn't about to ask. It was almost like thinking about his parents having sex, and that wasn't something he wanted to scar himself with for the rest of his life.

A knock on the door made Calum jerk up. Julian sighed and got his feet back on the floor.

"I was just starting to relax," he murmured.

"That will be Cynthia," Calum said as he rushed to the front door.

The healer had said she'd come around today. Initially, Julian and Kaspar had gone to her, but now, it was easier for everyone if she came to them.

Both pregnancies were going well, which was a relief. Calum wasn't sure what he'd do if something bad happened to either Kaspar or Julian. He felt closer to Julian, but that didn't mean he wasn't close to Kaspar. He'd decided he'd be their protector, and he took that job very seriously. That was why he made sure they had water and good food and didn't tire themselves too much. He was a bit like a mother hen, but neither of them had complained.

Calum suspected they enjoyed the attention. Neither of them had been loved much when they were younger, especially not Julian. Hell, he'd spent decades hiding in the forest, completely on his own except for his son. He deserved all the love in the world, and while Kaspar was there for that, Calum wasn't far behind. He loved Julian in a different way, but not any less.

He flung the door open, and sure enough, Cynthia stood there, waiting. She smiled and pushed past him, her focus already on her patients. "How are they today?" she asked.

"They're fine as far as I can tell. Kaspar is a bit annoyed that he has to spend most of his time on the couch, but I'm making sure he rests."

Cynthia nodded. She was carrying a bag that contained everything she'd need for the examinations. Her long skirt wrapped around her legs as she moved, and her graying hair was pulled up in a messy bun from which several strands had escaped. She looked kind, and she *was* kind.

Calum was always surprised when the badgers treated him as if he were one of them rather than a bat shifter. To them, it didn't make a difference that he hadn't been born in the cete. They'd welcomed all carriers, not caring what kind of shifters they were. The bat colony where Calum had grown up wouldn't have done that. In fact, they hadn't, and it wasn't just because their territory was surrounded by shifters from every side.

"I'm not surprised they're giving you trouble," Cynthia said. "This is when it starts getting frustrating for them."

Calum nodded. "I can only imagine." They'd been growing those babies for months now, and Calum had been there for all of it. He'd seen how Kaspar and Julian's bodies had changed and how they'd had to change their behavior to accommodate that. It sounded and looked incredibly frustrating, and he was glad he'd decided he didn't want children.

But that wasn't something he was willing to think about right now. Thinking about children made him think about the fact that he was a carrier, which he wanted to think about even less. He wasn't sure Cynthia would understand, anyway. Kaspar and Julian might, but Calum wasn't about to burden them with his feelings about children and being a carrier. They didn't hate what they were the way he did. He didn't fully understand it, especially after what Julian had gone through, but he'd keep these feelings to himself, especially considering that the babies were about to arrive.

"It's a good thing you decided to wait to have children," Cynthia said with a smile. "I can only imagine how this situation would be if you were pregnant, too."

Just the thought of getting pregnant made Calum feel queasy. "I don't even have a boyfriend," he pointed out.

"You don't need a boyfriend to have a child if you decide you want one."

"Maybe not, but it's the easiest way."

Cynthia winked. "Then I guess you should start looking for one."

There was nothing Calum wanted less. He was fine on his own, thank you very much. He was too busy taking care of Julian and Kaspar, and he couldn't afford for anyone to distract him from them, especially not a man.

Calum didn't need a man who'd expect him to carry his children just because he was a carrier. Kaspar and Julian were lucky they'd found each other and that both of them were carriers, but Calum had known too many men who wouldn't hesitate to force him to carry their child.

No, it was better for him to be on his own, and so what if sometimes, it made him feel lonely? He had Julian and Kaspar, and soon, their children. He wouldn't have the time to feel lonely once they arrived.

Duane took a bite of his sandwich as he scrolled down his phone. He hadn't expected that finding a job would be easy once he got out of the military, but he also hadn't expected it to be so hard. It looked like no one was hiring, and those who did were willing to pay him a pittance for his work. He might not be worth much, but he still needed a roof over his head and food in his stomach, dammit.

"How about security for someone?" his brother, Sheridan, asked as he stole one of Duane's fries from his plate.

Duane batted Sheridan's hand away. "Depends what kind of security," he said.

Sheridan grinned. "I see you doing well in a mall. Would they give you a uniform?"

Duane glared at his brother. "Why don't *you* go do security in a mall?"

"What, you think you're too good for that?"

Their father, Alan, sighed heavily. "Boys, no fighting at the dinner table."

"Is it the dinner table when we're having lunch?" Sheridan asked.

Duane went back to his scrolling. He needed to find a job, and soon. For now, he was living with his father, and while that was fine and his dad hadn't complained about it, Duane didn't want to stay here forever.

"Eat your sandwich," Alan ordered Sheridan.

It was good to be home. Duane had spent many years away from his family, which was one of the reasons he'd decided to leave the military behind. He was done with all of that, and he wanted to settle into his new life, but he wasn't sure how. Hell, he wasn't even sure what he wanted to do with his life now that he was free to live it.

There was only one thing he'd been trained to do, and that was fighting. He didn't want to continue in that line of work, but maybe Sheridan was right when he talked about security. It would be fairly easy to move from fighting to defending, and it was something Duane could see himself doing for a while, possibly the rest of his life.

There were lots of businesses and companies who would hire an ex-military for their security, but that didn't feel quite right. Duane wanted to make a real difference, and to do that, he'd have to go to people who couldn't afford to hire someone to protect them. Of course, that would be a problem because Duane needed to eat and pay rent, which meant he had to get paid.

Everything had been easier when he'd been in the military.

He continued looking through job listings as he ate. His brother and father were bickering, but it didn't bother him. If anything, it made him feel good. He was home, and he was never leaving again.

His eyes caught on one of the listings. He frowned and clicked on it, unsure what to think as he started reading.

"The shifters in the Allegheny forest are looking for guards," he said.

That stopped the bickering faster than anything else could have.

"You want to work with shifters?" Sheridan asked. He didn't sound disgusted like many people would have been, which was a relief.

Duane shrugged. "No idea."

"But you're reading the posting. That means that it appeals to you in some way."

Duane couldn't deny it. If shifters were looking for guards, it meant they needed them. It was odd that they were looking for human guards, but Duane had heard about things changing in the forest, and he was curious.

He'd always been curious. He and his family lived close to the forest. His parents had never been afraid of shifters, and when the shifters had been locked away in their forests, they'd decided they wouldn't move. Even after Duane's mother died, his father had finished raising him and Sheridan in the house where they'd been brought as newborns. Alan was never leaving, and Duane liked that.

He'd always liked having a home to return to, and finding work in the forest meant he'd be close enough to visit his father anytime he wanted. He had a lot of questions about the job, but he couldn't deny he was tempted.

He'd been surprised at the listing, but he was even more surprised when he continued reading. "They want someone who's willing to live in the forest with the shifters."

Sheridan sucked in a breath. "There are no humans in the forest."

"Maybe there are, and we don't know about them."

Alan finished his sandwich and bundled up the wrapping in his hand. "I've heard about a human team living there," he said. "Military people."

How had Duane not heard about them? He supposed he wouldn't have unless he'd asked, and he hadn't. He'd tried to put as much distance as he could between himself and his old job, but it sounded like he shouldn't have. Maybe if he hadn't, he'd know what was happening.

"So you think this is legit?"

"Pretty sure it is, but you won't find out if you don't apply, will you?"

Duane looked from his father to his brother. "You think I should?"

"I don't see why not," Alan said.

"Most people wouldn't apply," Sheridan pointed out.

"But your brother isn't most people. Besides, we've lived here all your lives, and nothing bad ever happened. I don't think you'd be good for that job, but Duane? As long as he can protect someone, he'll be happy."

Sheridan scowled and crossed his arms over his chest. "You don't think I could protect those people?"

"I have no doubt you'd try, but you'd get yourself in trouble, and fast. You'd probably knock up a pretty shifter and start a diplomatic incident or something."

Duane laughed. "He's not wrong."

"You two don't know me as well as you clearly think you do," Sheridan said.

Sometimes Duane felt like he didn't know his brother anymore, but that was why he was here. He wanted to get to know his father and brother again and truly become part of their lives. "You've always been a troublemaker."

"I'm an adult now. I don't create trouble."

"Don't you?" Alan drawled. "Why, I remember a few weeks ago, Mrs. Williams told me that I had to keep you away from her daughter."

Sheridan's cheeks flushed. "Eliza is an adult, and she can make her own decisions. Besides, we're not together."

"That's good to hear. Maybe I won't have to fight off Mrs. Williams after all."

If Duane remembered right, Eliza was in her early twenties, while Sheridan was thirty-five. Maybe that was why Mrs. Williams wasn't happy about Sheridan nosing around her daughter. Duane didn't see anything wrong with an age difference, but he wasn't Mrs. Williams.

Still, he was glad that things weren't that serious between Sheridan and Eliza. Sheridan was nice, even though sometimes he behaved like he was still in his twenties rather than his thirties. He didn't deserve for anyone to look down on him, especially not for something as ridiculous as his age.

Of course, Duane could be wrong about why Mrs. Williams didn't like Sheridan.

"You'll apply?" Sheridan asked, clearly eager to change the topic of the conversation.

Duane shrugged. "I can certainly try. I won't make any decisions before I know what they expect me to do, but it looks like a good job." And the pay was decent.

"Even though they'll expect you to move into the forest?"

That tidbit was exciting. Duane had always wondered what the forest was like, and if he took this job, he'd be one of the few humans to find out. "It's not that far from the house and your apartment. I could still visit."

"If they let you."

Duane frowned. "I don't see why they shouldn't. If humans had put out this job offer, I wouldn't hesitate. Everything looks good on paper."

"But maybe it won't be good in reality. People have been grumbling about shifters possibly being allowed to leave their forests. I bet there are protests more often than we're aware of in front of their gates."

Duane was afraid of that, but he decided to apply anyway. He could refuse the job if he didn't like the offer they made, but he'd have put himself out there in the meantime. He didn't want to squander this opportunity, especially since it sounded like humans were harassing the forest shifters.

Duane had always been a protector. He'd fought for his country for years, and shifters were part of the country, even though some people didn't view them as such. Duane saw things differently, and he'd fight for them if they needed him to.

Chapter Two

Calum stared at the fridge. It was empty, much more than it should be, dammit. How could he have allowed it to get to this point? He needed to feed Kaspar and Julian, and he wasn't going to be able to do that when the only things in the fridge were a lemon, a carton of milk, and some yogurt.

He sighed and closed the door. He knew why he'd been putting off going to the grocery store, but he couldn't do it any longer. It was almost time for lunch, so Julian and Kaspar would get hungry soon. They'd no doubt offer to go out and get something to eat, but they could barely walk by this point. They couldn't see their feet, and they didn't have the best balance.

Calum realized he was being a mother hen again, but he didn't want to put Julian and Kaspar in danger. It was better for them to stay home, where they were comfortable, and that meant that Calum would have to go to the grocery store on his own.

He sucked in a breath. He could do it. It wouldn't be the first time he did, and it no doubt wouldn't be the last. He'd learned how to drive for this reason, and even though driving still made him nervous, he could do it.

For Julian and Kaspar.

Wasting time wouldn't make this easier, so he went to look for the two of them. They were on the couch like most days, cuddling together as they watched TV. Kaspar had an arm around Julian's shoulders and was rubbing his thigh with his other hand.

They both appeared a bit guilty when they noticed Calum, and Kaspar snatched his hand away from Julian's leg.

Calum rolled his eyes. "You don't have to act as if I'm your father. I don't care what the two of you get up to, especially when I'm not here. As long as you don't push yourself too much and go into labor because of it."

Julian laughed. "We'll make sure neither of us goes into labor while you're out. You're going to the grocery store?"

Calum nodded. "We need food. Is there anything the two of you want in particular?"

Calum made a list so he wouldn't forget anything. He walked around the house before heading out, adding more items to the list until he was satisfied he'd thought of everything.

Then he left.

Thomas had been more than happy to help Calum learn how to drive and give him a car. Calum had made sure to tell him it was only for Kaspar and Julian's benefit, which Thomas hadn't seemed to like. Sometimes, it was hard to understand how the alpha thought.

Calum's old alpha had never been as selfless and welcoming as Thomas. Calum realized his life could have been much worse. He'd lived with the carriers in the Bishop house long enough to know everyone's history and what they'd gone through. Next to some of them, Calum had been incredibly lucky. He'd never been abused or raped and had never been forced to carry a child he didn't want. He hadn't been treated great, but it was nothing compared to the others, and he felt guilty feeling bad for it.

But Thomas and the rest of the badgers had never treated him any differently than they treated the other carriers, which, to Calum's surprise, had been as if they weren't different from every other shifter.

Most shifters thought carriers were nothing more than

baby-making machines and looked at them like objects or something they didn't want anything to do with. Calum's old alpha belonged in the first group. Calum wasn't sure he would have forced him into anything, but he was glad he'd never have to find out.

No matter how nervous Calum was at the thought of driving, it usually faded once he got on the road, and today wasn't any different. By the time he reached the grocery store just outside badger territory, he was humming along with the radio and thrumming his fingers on the steering wheel. Parking always made him sweat, but luckily for him, there weren't many people in the grocery store, and the parking lot was mostly empty. It was easy for him to find a good spot and leave the car there, and once he was out of the car, he grinned at himself.

He'd been sheltered with the colony, but not anymore. Now that he lived with the badgers and the laws had changed, he was like any other shifter, and he could do whatever he wanted. He didn't particularly enjoy grocery shopping, but he did enjoy taking care of Kaspar and Julian, and grocery shopping was part of that.

He grabbed a cart and started his shopping. He went through his entire list, making sure he didn't forget anything and adding a few things he hadn't thought about earlier. He was getting more milk when he felt someone stop behind him. He ignored them, thinking they'd go away, but when he could still feel their presence, he turned with a frown on his face.

His heart froze, and he couldn't do anything but stare at his old alpha.

The man smiled. "Calum. I didn't expect to see you at the grocery store," Foley said.

Calum would never think of the man as his alpha again. Thomas was his alpha now, and while Foley hadn't done anything to hurt Calum, Calum didn't trust him or his smile. "I have to eat just like everyone else," he pointed out.

"True. That looks like a lot of food just for you, though." Foley looked down at the cart, which was full.

"It's not just for me," Calum said, but he didn't mention Julian and Kaspar.

Foley's eyes narrowed, even though he was still smiling. "Isn't it? Does that mean you have a family now? I haven't heard from you since you refused to come home, and some-times, I worry."

Calum's mouth was dry. He should have known it wouldn't be as easy as refusing to go back to the colony. "You have nothing to worry about. I'm perfectly fine, and besides, you're not my alpha anymore."

"I might not be your alpha, but you were part of the colony for your entire life. How can I not worry about you?"

Foley stepped closer. Calum tried moving away, but there was nowhere for him to go. He was stuck between his cart, the aisle behind him, and Foley.

Foley didn't come close enough to touch Calum, but he might as well have. The urge to shift was strong, but Calum wouldn't run away this time. He had to remember that he was part of the cete now. If anything happened to him, Thomas would find him and get him back. He was a better man than Foley could ever be.

"Have you thought about coming home?" Foley asked.

"I'm already home."

"The badgers aren't your family, no matter what they told you. What did they offer you to stay with them?"

"Nothing. I'm staying with the badgers because I want to."

"So you were abandoning us just like that? The colony has been your home for your entire life. Don't you think you owe it to us to come back and be useful?"

Calum could too easily imagine what use Foley would find

for him. It made the panic grow in his chest to the point that he wasn't sure he'd be able to stop himself from shifting if Foley insisted.

"Your place has always been with us," Foley continued. "I'm sure you'll see that once you come back."

"What's going on here?" a strong voice asked from behind Foley.

Foley stepped away, and Calum could breathe again. When he saw Kari standing there with his son strapped against his chest, he could have kissed him. Julian's son had saved him, and Calum suspected he knew that.

"It's none of your business," Foley snapped.

"It is when you're harassing one of my friends. Calum? Are you done?"

Calum grabbed the cart and pushed it past Foley. "I have more stuff to grab."

Kari squeezed Calum's shoulder. "Then we can finish grocery shopping together. It's not my favorite activity, and I could do with a friend as I finish up."

Foley was still standing there, staring at Calum. It sent a shiver down Calum's spine.

He had no doubt his old alpha was planning something. The problem was that he didn't know what.

The feeling of his feet pounding on the asphalt was soothing to Duane. His left calf hurt a bit, but it was nothing he couldn't run through. As he jogged, he listened to one of his favorite podcasts, wondering how some human beings could be so cruel. True crime wasn't for everyone, but while Duane didn't enjoy listening to the more gruesome details, he thought it helped him understand people better. It also made sense that he wanted to protect people, especially shifters, who were even more vulnerable. They were locked in their forests and viewed as monsters, something Duane had never agreed with.

And now, people were campaigning to keep the shifters there, restrained and vulnerable.

Duane hadn't been born yet when humans had found out about shifters and had decided to stick them in the forests. He didn't understand the reasons behind that decision and didn't think he would have even if he'd been alive then.

The problem was that he didn't know any shifter personally. Most humans didn't, since shifters were confined to their forests. Maybe they were monsters as some humans said, but Duane didn't believe it. As far as he knew, shifters were just humans who could turn into animals. The thought was awe-inspiring and incredible, but not scary, at least not to him.

But he understood why it might be to some people. That didn't mean shifters were evil. People were always afraid of what they didn't know, which meant that the best way to get rid of that fear would be for humans to get to know shifters. That wasn't possible if they couldn't leave the forests, and Duane had no idea if the depictions of shifters in movies and TV series were correct. How could he know?

How could anyone know?

His phone vibrated in the pouch at his waist, and he struggled to get it out. If it was his brother or his father, they wouldn't care if he answered while running, but he didn't recognize the number that flashed on the screen, so he slowed down, then started walking.

"Yes?"

"Duane Walsh?" a man asked.

"Yes, it's me."

"My name is Luther Mallory. You applied for a job in the Allegheny forest."

Duane sucked in a breath. He hadn't expected anyone to call him back, especially not so quickly. He'd only applied a few days ago. "I did."

"I'm in charge of hiring the guards. Well, my team and I are. I was surprised to see your application."

"Why?" Duane used his hand to mop away some of the sweat dripping from his forehead.

"Because of your experience in the military. I'd expect someone like you to want a different kind of job."

"Well, I'd be fine with less hurting people and more helping them, which is why I thought this job looked good. I understand if I'm not what you're looking for, though." Althhough why would he have called?

"To be honest, only a few people have applied, nowhere near the number of guards we need. Some of those people weren't fit for the job, but you are, Mr. Walsh."

"Thank you." Duane hadn't expected to get the job.

"Of course, considering the type of job it is and where you'll be working, I expect you to want to know everything and see the forest before you accept and sign the contract. I have to warn you that your job won't be an easy one. The forest has seen protesters in the past few weeks, and some of them are incredibly angry. They've been harassing anyone who enters and exits the forest, but all of those people are human. The protesters have also been trying to get to the shifters. They're doing so by climbing our fences and injuring themselves. So far, shifters have been safe, but I'm afraid it won't last forever."

"I've seen the news. What are you trying to tell me, Mr. Mallory?" Duane was pretty sure that wasn't Mallory's title, but the man hadn't offered anything else.

"Please, call me Luther. If you take the job, we'll be working closely, and I want us to be comfortable."

"All right, Luther, but please, call me Duane. I have to be honest. It sounds like you're trying to make me change my mind about working in the forest."

"I'm not. We need you and the other people who applied. I just don't want to start losing people once you get here and see what the job is about. Besides, you also have to be comfortable around shifters and be open to the possibility of permanently moving to the forest if things work out. This isn't a temporary job. Can you see yourself living in the forest? Meeting shifters, befriending them, and possibly creating a family with one of them?"

"To be honest, I hadn't thought that far."

"Maybe you should. Do you have a family? I see on your application that you're not married."

"Only my brother and my father, and they're okay with me moving to the forest and taking the job. Can you give me more details? Where would I be living?" Now that Duane knew he'd have to guard the shifters and their forest against humans trying to get to them, he had a better idea of what Luther was looking for and was convinced he could do it. He was also curious about everything else.

"For now, we're placing the guards in territories that border the edge of the forest, so you'll be in one of those. You can choose to live in the town at the center of the forest, but it would make your job more complicated, since you'd have to commute."

Like everyone, Duane had an idea of how the forest had been divided. There were many kinds of shifters living there, and each of them had their own territory. That was pretty much all Duane knew, though. "Where would you place me?"

"I was thinking of the badgers, considering your application. Thomas will be delighted to have you on board and offer you your own house if that's what you want. For a start, you'll be living with the other guards, but it won't be for long. If you decide to stay, you can build a life here."

"Is that what you've done?" Because there was no way

anyone had put a shifter in charge of hiring guards. That meant Luther was human, but he spoke as if he were part of the forest, almost a shifter himself. If he was building himself a life there, it would make sense.

There was a moment of silence. Duane thought that maybe he'd pushed too much and that Luther was about to tell him that things wouldn't work out after all, but instead, the man sighed.

"It is. My team and I were sent here to find out more about the infighting between the alphas and the various kinds of shifters. I met someone here."

"So you live in the forest permanently?"

"I do. Even if I were to lose my job, this is my home now."

And maybe, it could become Duane's home.

"Do you have questions?" Luther asked.

Duane had too many of them to ask them on the phone. "Just one big one. Why are you doing this? I mean, you told me why the guards are necessary, so I understand that part, but why haven't you been putting shifters by the fences? It's their territory. Shouldn't they be the ones defending it?"

"They should be, and they're eager to do so. How would it look if a shifter had to wound or even kill a human, though? No one would care if the human had been trespassing and maybe even planning on hurting shifters."

That much was true. Duane could tell there was more to the situation, but he was fine with that answer for now. "I still want the job," he told Luther because he was pretty sure that was what the man was waiting for.

"That's good."

Duane didn't think he imagined the relief in Luther's tone.

"I'll send over the contract. You'll see there's a trial period of two months for you to start with. If you're still convinced you want to do this, we'll be happy to have you on board permanently. If you decide it's too much for you or not what you're looking for, you'll be allowed to leave without anyone stopping you. Welcome on board."

Something told Duane he wouldn't be leaving, but there was no way for him to be sure until he got there.

And he couldn't wait.

"I was just saying hello," Foley said.

He wasn't giving up easily, but Calum hadn't expected him to.

"Well, you said hello, and now, you can say goodbye," Kari said. He bared his teeth in the creepiest smile Calum had ever seen.

"Calum was my colony member his entire life. Surely, you don't expect me not to care about him?"

Calum wanted to run away screaming, but he wasn't willing to give Foley that much power over him. He couldn't afford for his old alpha to see how much he still impacted him, so he worked hard to keep his expression the same.

He didn't think Foley would grab him and drag him back to the colony. He wouldn't do that in front of other people, and while the grocery store was far from full, it wasn't empty. Calum could tell Foley was planning something, though, and he had no doubt it involved him. From what Foley had said, he wanted Calum to come home, which meant that was his goal. He was trying to find a way to make it happen, and Calum could imagine all the scenarios he was coming up with.

He didn't like any of them.

"Oh, I'm sure you care," Kari said, taking a step toward Foley. "But it doesn't matter. Calum is the master of his own life and decided to stay with the badgers. That means he's not your problem or your colony member to worry over anymore. *Thomas* is his alpha, and he'll take care of him. If that was what you were afraid of, you shouldn't be. Calum will be just fine, and he'll finally be happy."

Foley opened his mouth, but Calum was done with this. He grabbed Kari's hand and pulled, thankful when Kari turned his attention to him.

"We have things to do," Calum said.

"Better things than talking to me?" Foley sounded offended, which wasn't a surprise.

Calum didn't care how Foley felt. He hoped he'd never see the man again but suspected that wouldn't be the case. His stomach already churned as he thought about the next time he'd see him, but he decided he'd worry about it when the time came. For now, he was going to finish his grocery shopping, bring everything back to Kaspar and Julian, and get lunch ready for them. Once they were napping, he could break down and obsess over what Foley would do.

Kari gave a little growl when Foley tried to stop them, but Calum pulled him along. Foley even reached for him but seemed to think better of it when two elderly women turned the corner and walked down the aisle they were standing in. Calum could feel his gaze on his back as he moved, but he didn't turn to look, and neither did Kari.

"Why are all alphas assholes?" Kari asked. He was fuming, and if Calum had been anyone else, he'd have been worried Kari might hurt him.

Kari was the closest thing to a vigilante the forest had. Calum wasn't sure if he was retired now that he had a partner and a child, but he wouldn't want to find out the wrong way. He'd never killed anyone who didn't deserve it as far as Calum knew, but Calum thought Kari would be willing to change that if it meant Foley would stop bothering him.

"Thomas isn't an asshole, and neither is Morris. There's also Josiah," Calum pointed out.

Kari turned narrowed eyes at him. "You know what I

mean."

"I do, and I agree that most alphas in the forest were assholes, but we're changing that, right?"

Kari sighed heavily and nodded. "We are, and I didn't mean them. I hate that guy, though."

"I can't say I'm his biggest fan."

Kari cocked his head. "Has he hurt you? Is that why you refused to return to the colony after it was safe?"

Calum quickly shook his head. He didn't want people to think he'd been abused. He'd lived with people who had been, and he knew how much it hurt them. He didn't need the kind of attention that had been given to them. "He never raised a hand to me or anyone else as far as I know."

Kari didn't seem convinced. "Abuse isn't only physical."

"I'm aware of that, but I'm fine. I promise."

"As long as you know that you can come to me if you need anything." Kari leaned closer. "And I do mean *anything*."

Calum swallowed. He was pretty sure Kari had just offered to kill Foley for him, but he wasn't about to ask. He was kind of scared that Kari would turn around, go back to Foley, and kill him right here in the grocery store.

Hopefully, his son's presence would keep him calm.

Calum peered at the sleeping baby. He'd never wanted children, and he hadn't changed his mind, but he was about to start raising two children. He wouldn't be the babies' father, but he was glad for that. He didn't want that kind of responsibility, and seeing what Kaspar and Julian had gone through didn't make him want to get pregnant. He was fine as he was, and he doubted he'd ever change his mind.

But even if he didn't, he'd soon have the care of two babies, and he didn't know how to deal with that. He'd been around small children, but this would be the first time he wasn't trying to avoid them.

"Do you want to take him?" Kari suddenly asked.

Calum took a step back as if it had been a threat. "No, thank you."

Kari arched a brow. He didn't look murderous anymore, which was a step forward. "You didn't have to react as if I'd asked you to carry a bomb."

"He's sleeping. I don't want to wake him up."

"Maybe I should. I swear, he sleeps half an hour in the afternoon, then goes on until past midnight."

"Is that something I have to worry about?"

"You mean for my father's and Kaspar's children?"

Calum nodded. "Yeah. I've decided to take the night shifts, especially in the beginning."

"I'm not sure that will work. They have to feed the kids, even during the night."

"We'll find a way to make it work."

"And that's why they love you."

Calum wasn't sure about that, but he was still glad for Kari's words. After all, Kari was Julian's son. He knew his father better than anyone, possibly even better than Kaspar. For many years, it had been them against the world. Calum couldn't even begin to imagine what that had been like, and he didn't want to try.

Maybe he did isolate himself, but if he wanted to spend time with other people, he could easily do so. He hadn't been spending most of his time in his bedroom since he'd moved in with Julian and Kaspar, anyway.

But Julian and Kari had truly been alone in the world. Julian had raised Kari on his own in the forest, hiding in fear that if he was found, his alpha would take Kari away. Knowing what he did of the situation, Calum agreed it had been a possibility.

But now, both Julian and Kari were out of the deep forest. They lived with the badgers, were both fathers, and were happy. It gave Calum hope, although he wasn't sure what he wanted from his future. For now, he was fine just thinking about it. Maybe when the children were grown up, he'd finally know what he wanted to do.

"You know, you don't have to be an island," Kari said.

"I'm pretty sure I'm not."

Kari rolled his eyes. "You know what I mean. Your entire time at the Bishop house, you behaved as if no one could understand you. That might be true because we don't know what you went through, but it doesn't mean we don't understand and that we don't care about you. I do, and my father does, too. He's willing to trust you with his children, and that's not something he does lightly."

Calum's eyes burned, but he refused to cry. He didn't want to expose how fragile he was, especially to Kari, who was the strongest carrier Calum had ever known.

Or maybe not. Julian had been strong, as had Philip, Micah, and so many of them. That was one of the reasons Calum had stayed away from them. How could he compare himself to them when his life had been so nice?

He'd always had a home, and while people had treated him differently after finding out he was a carrier, no one had ever hurt him. He hadn't been abused, beaten, or raped. He hadn't been forced to marry someone he didn't want or to get pregnant. Any of the carriers he'd lived with before would have given anything to be in his place, so what did he have to complain about?

Kari sighed. "Just think about it. Everyone needs people, including you and me. It took me a while to realize that, but now that I have, I can't imagine my life without the man I love and my son. I don't know what happened to you, but you deserve to be happy, no matter what that means to you."

Calum might deserve it, but he didn't even know himself what happiness would look like for him.

After hanging up with Luther, Duane ran home. It was odd to think that he wouldn't be living in the house he'd grown up in in just a few days. It was different from the apartments he'd lived in while he worked for the government, and part of him was sorry to leave it behind. Another part was eager to start a new life, full of possibilities and opportunities. This place would always be home, but maybe he could find a new home somewhere else, in the forest.

And wasn't that a surprise.

He couldn't imagine his life in the forest, but he'd find out how it would be soon enough. He didn't see a problem with living with shifters. After all, they were human beings as much as he was. He expected to see animals more often, but not wild ones. That was all the difference there would be, as far as he was concerned, and he couldn't wait to start working.

When Duane reached home, his father was in his workshop at the back of the house. Duane waved at him, hesitated, then decided to shower before talking to him. He could have gone right away, but he was dripping with sweat, and he wouldn't inflict that on anyone, least of all his father.

But he rushed through his shower, eager to tell his dad what was going on. Alan knew Duane had applied for the job, and he'd even pushed him in that direction. Hopefully, it meant he approved of Duane moving into the forest and protecting shifters.

No one in their family ever had anything to say against shifters. Duane's father had known several of them before they were locked away, and he'd always talked about them with fondness. They'd been childhood friends, people who hadn't deserved to be taken away from their homes just because of what they were. Duane couldn't do anything to fix what had been done to them, but he could do everything in his power to make their life easier and safer.

By the time he got downstairs, his father was in the kitchen, washing his hands.

"Good run?" Alan asked.

Duane took a bottle of water from the fridge and sat at the kitchen table. "It was. I got a call back from that job in the forest."

Duane's father turned to look at him. "I take it that's a good thing?"

"How do you know?"

"You're smiling."

Duane was, and he hadn't even realized it. "I didn't think they'd call me back, to be honest. I'm a little surprised."

"But you won't change your mind about going."

"No. I want to do this. Those shifters are in danger, and I can help them. Why shouldn't I?"

"I'm not saying you shouldn't. I just worry, but then, I always will."

"The shifters won't hurt me." Duane was sure of that, although he could be wrong. He hoped he wouldn't be.

"They're not the only people who might hurt you, though. I've seen the news. They showed the protests and even mentioned that some people have tried climbing the fences. You'll be protecting those, and I can't help but worry about what will happen if someone brings a gun to this fight."

Duane understood, but he was used to throwing himself into danger when it was the last thing someone else would do. "I was trained to deal with guns, remember?"

"And you need to remember that you're my son and that I'll always worry about you."

"How about I promise to text or call every day and visit you every week?"

Alan chuckled. "It would help, but I don't want to be a bother. For years, we went weeks without hearing from you.

I can deal with that for a while longer."

But Duane didn't want him to. That was one of the reasons he'd left the military. While he worked for the government, he hadn't been allowed to call his family nearly as often as he'd wanted. He understood the reasoning behind that, but it had been hard on him and his family.

Duane wasn't a soldier anymore. He was free to call his father whenever he wanted and tell him about his day, and that was what he was planning on doing. Hopefully, Luther wouldn't have a problem with that, but it was something Duane would need to ask. He wanted to be prepared when it came to what would greet him when he got to the forest and what Luther and the shifters who lived there expected from him.

His father grabbed his shoulder and squeezed. "I'm proud of you."

Duane choked just a bit. "Thank you."

"When your mother passed away, I wasn't sure how I'd deal with raising two children. I was sure it would be a disaster and that you'd end up hating me, and I'm glad to see that's not the case."

"I could never hate you, and I know Sheridan feels the same."

"Well, that's good. I'm glad you found a job you're happy with. I've watched you since you came home, and I know how much you hate feeling useless and having nothing to do. This ought to change that, and seeing how excited you are makes me feel better. I'm not saying I'll stop worrying, but I have faith in you and your abilities. As long as you're happy, I'm happy, too."

"Well, I don't know how this will go, but I feel better than I have in a long time."

Duane's father dropped his hand. "Then you're doing the right thing."

Duane hoped he was. He hadn't changed his mind about going to the forest, and he was excited, but the job might not be for him. He might not be able to deal with living with shifters, or maybe he'd be too homesick, although he didn't see how that could be a problem considering his past job experience. He wouldn't know about any of this until he started working, though, and even though there was a bit of fear, his strongest feeling was excitement.

He'd found a job, and he'd finally be useful again. He'd be able to find out what happened in the forest, something few humans could say. He'd be living with shifters, be tasked with keeping them safe, and be paid for it.

Really, what more could he want?

CHAPTER THREE

"Do we still have some peanut butter and chocolate ice cream?" Kaspar asked.

He looked hopeful, and Calum hated to disappoint him. "You finished it last night."

Kaspar's smile vanished. "Oh. I didn't realize that was the last of it. Well, I suppose I can have something else. Do we have vanilla?"

"We do." But Calum knew that wasn't Kaspar's favorite or what Kaspar was craving. Kaspar's pregnancy might be almost over, but it didn't mean the cravings were gone, and Calum wanted to help him deal with them.

But the peanut butter and chocolate ice cream was gone. The only way to get more would be to go to the grocery store, something Calum had been avoiding over the past week.

He realized it was ridiculous. Last week hadn't been the first time he went to the grocery store, but it had been the only time he'd seen Foley there. Every other trip to the store had been fine, and Foley's presence had to have been a coincidence. There was no way Calum would see him again if he went, and he needed to get over his fear and unexplainable panic and just go.

Kaspar turned toward the kitchen, but Calum gently touched his elbow. "How about I go to the store and get you the ice cream you actually want?"

"I'm fine with vanilla," Kaspar insisted.

Calum had no doubt Kaspar would eat the vanilla ice cream. He was nice and kind, just like Julian. They were the

29

perfect match, and sometimes, watching them together made Calum's heart feel like it was breaking. He was happy for them, but he wanted the same for himself, and he didn't see how he could get it.

Of course, being stuck in a house with two heavily pregnant men wasn't helping him meet people. Maybe another trip to the grocery store wasn't such a bad idea. He'd never heard about anyone finding their soulmate at the grocery store, but he was willing to be the first to do so.

"Go sit down on the couch, maybe put on that movie you were planning on watching. I'll run to the grocery store and be back before you even realize I was gone. I'll even bring back *two* cartons of ice cream."

"You spoil us."

"You deserve to be spoiled, and there's no better time to do so than right now." Calum gestured at Kaspar's stomach.

Sometimes, during the evenings the three of them spent watching TV together, Calum could see a tiny hand or foot press against Kaspar and Julian's stomachs. It was weird because their stomachs turned into pointy things, but it reminded Calum that babies were growing in them.

Honestly, it creeped him out a bit.

He couldn't imagine himself being pregnant, and most of the process felt weird. Julian and Kaspar were happy, though, and that was all that mattered in the end. If there was anything Calum could do to make this easier on them, he'd do it, and that included going to the grocery store.

He gently guided Kaspar back toward the living room, helped him settle on the couch, and made sure he had everything he needed. Julian was already there and seemed amused, but he didn't point out that Calum was mothering them. They were probably glad he was going to the grocery store because he'd stop hovering for at least an hour.

Calum couldn't imagine not doing so. He was terrified that

something would happen to Julian or Kaspar and that he wouldn't be able to do anything to stop it. That was why he was indulging them, and he wouldn't stop.

"I'll be right back," he promised before heading out.

Because he was so anxious over Foley, it was easy to ignore the nervousness over driving when he climbed into the car, drove to the store, and parked. There were more people in the parking lot this time, but he took a deep breath and slid his car between two of those already there. He was a bit too much to the right, but hopefully, the car there would be gone by the time he left the store.

He grabbed a cart, mentally making a list of what he'd need. He kept an eye on the parking lot, hoping he wouldn't see Foley's car. He was relieved when he didn't and got into the store without bumping into his old alpha.

He was tense the entire time he shopped. Every time he turned a corner, he expected to see Foley there, but the alpha never was. Calum managed to get everything he wanted, including two cartons of peanut butter and chocolate ice cream. He was smiling by the time he reached the checkout counter, but the smile froze when he looked up from putting things on the belt and crossed gazes with someone he remembered too well, and not for a good reason.

Rip looked Calum up and down, then dismissed him as if they hadn't dated for a year. He turned away, tapping his foot impatiently.

Rip had always been impatient. When he'd asked Calum out, Calum hadn't been sure what to say, so Rip had pushed. It was Rip who'd decided what they did on their dates, and he'd been the one to insist when they had sex the first time. He always wanted more, at least until he'd realized that Calum was a carrier.

Calum's family had known, as well as Foley, but it wasn't something anyone wanted to get out, especially when the laws hadn't been what they were now. Calum hadn't known how Rip would react when he told him, but after a while, he'd felt his boyfriend needed to know and hoped Rip would take it well.

Calum wished he'd never said the words. Rip had freaked out and asked Calum if he was pregnant. Even after Calum told him that he wasn't, Rip broke up with him. Calum had never been quite sure why Rip had panicked so badly when he'd dated girls before. They could get pregnant, too, yet, he hadn't had a problem with that.

But he did have a problem with Calum.

"I'm surprised the badgers let you out of their sight," Rip muttered.

Even though he wasn't looking at Calum, Calum had no doubt he was talking to him.

Once, he'd have cowered and let Rip berate him. He wasn't willing to do that now, even though he was terrified. Surely his ex-boyfriend wouldn't beat him up in the middle of the grocery store. "Why shouldn't they?" he asked, hoping his voice didn't betray how nervous he was.

Rip turned to look at him again. "You're a carrier."

"So?" Did Rip really have to say that as if Calum was carrying a deadly disease? It wasn't like Rip could become a carrier just because he was in the same room as Calum.

"You're a freak," Rip spat out, clearly not caring if the people around them could hear him. "You shouldn't have been allowed out of the colony, and if the badger alpha knows what's good for him, he'll keep you locked up."

There was so much hatred and venom in Rip's tone that Calum was stunned. He didn't understand what he'd done to make Rip hate him the way he did.

"You didn't have a problem with me going around when you dated me," he pointed out.

"I didn't know what you were. Freaks like you shouldn't

be allowed to date. I don't understand how people can want your kind." He looked Calum up and down again. "Although I'm ready to bet that no one wants *you*."

It was too close to the pain Calum carried every day. Yes, he pushed everyone away, but it wasn't because he wanted to be alone, at least not entirely. It was easier to push people away before they rejected him like Rip had.

Calum had thought Rip loved him. He'd been wrong and wasn't willing to take the risk again.

Duane was at the back of the line at the checkout, minding his own business and scrolling down his phone.

He'd arrived in the forest a few days ago and was still trying to get his bearings. He'd been taken to a big house he now shared with the other guards, and Luther had explained that the various alphas were still setting things up for the guards. For now, it was easier to keep all of them in the same spot, but that would change soon.

Duane liked most of the guards he was living with. It was odd to be living with so many people again, but he was used to it, so it wasn't a problem. He'd decided to explore the area today, which was how he'd stumbled onto this grocery store. It was small but clean and quaint, and it looked like it belonged in a small town.

Duane supposed it *was* in a small town.

Luther had explained that while there was a proper city in the center of the forest, most of the packs had smaller towns with stores and whatever else the pack and the members might need. This town was shared among several shifter groups, and as Duane shopped, he couldn't help but wonder what kind of shifters the people around him were. He knew better than to ask, and considering that these people didn't know he was human, he didn't want to bring attention to himself. Luther had said that while they were trying to open up the forest, not all shifters were okay with that, and Duane didn't want to stumble onto someone who thought that way.

But even though he'd decided not to draw attention, he was going to have to, because there was no way he wouldn't step in after hearing the conversation happening in front of him. He wasn't the only one who'd heard what the two guys were saying, but everyone else was looking away as if it was none of their business. Duane supposed it wasn't, but that wouldn't be enough to keep him away when the first guy was so rude. His words had made Duane angry, and while he couldn't see the expression of the second guy because he had his back to him, there was no way anyone would take those words easily. Duane didn't even have to know what a carrier was to understand the first guy was using it as an insult.

He smiled at the middle-aged woman standing in front of him and gestured. "Can I pass?"

She looked from him to the two men still discussing. "Are you going to do something about that?"

"If I can."

She nodded and stepped aside to let him pass. He did so with a smile and a thank you nod, then focused on the situation.

The guy who had his back to him was on the smaller side, at least next to Duane's six foot three height. The fact that he was also incredibly thin didn't help, but Duane could see he wasn't actually that small, just a few inches shorter than the guy he was talking to. He had messy black hair, and when he turned to see who was standing behind him, Duane noticed his dark eyes. His skin was pale, although it might look like that because of how dark his eyes and hair were.

"Hey," Duane said.

He wasn't sure how to intervene, but that wouldn't stop him from doing so.

"What the fuck do you want?" the other guy snapped.

He was blond with brown eyes, and his cheeks were flushed. He looked pissed, but then, he'd looked that way since he and the smaller guy had started talking.

"Do you really have to be rude?" the cute dark-haired guy asked.

"Stay out of this."

To Duane's surprise, the dark-haired guy grabbed his arm before he could say anything. "You're being rude to my boyfriend, and I should stay out of it?"

That gave the other guy pause. "Your boyfriend?"

"Yes. You have a problem with that?"

Duane had no idea what was happening, but clearly this guy needed him to be his boyfriend for the next ten minutes. He had no problem with that, but he had no doubt that the guy was freaking out internally. Duane knew he would if he were in the guy's situation.

He put the few things he was carrying onto the belt and wrapped his arm around his new boyfriend's waist. "I'm Duane," he said.

Instead of giving him his name, the rude guy glared at him. "Why are you dating Calum?"

Duane was glad he had his new boyfriend's name. He probably wouldn't see Calum again once they were out of the store, but it would help him not say something stupid. "Why shouldn't I?" He hoped Calum wasn't dating this asshole.

"Because of what he is. How can you stand that?"

Duane had no idea what Calum was, but he wouldn't have cared even if they had been dating. He looked down at Calum, whose eyes were wide and who was looking from Duane to the asshole. "How do you know this guy?" he asked.

"He's my ex-boyfriend. Remember, I told you about him."

At least he was an ex. Duane didn't understand how

Calum had dated him, but it wasn't his place to judge. "Right. I just hadn't realized he'd be so . . ."

Duane wasn't sure how to finish that sentence. The ex-boyfriend was an asshole, rude, and didn't deserve Calum. Duane was sure of that, even though he didn't know Calum.

The woman behind the checkout cleared her throat, and the three of them looked at her. The ex-boyfriend's cheeks flushed even redder, and he turned to focus on her, but Duane didn't miss how he kept peeking at him and Calum. The show wasn't over yet, so he made sure to lean into it.

He still had his arm wrapped around Calum's waist, and he pressed closer, a smile playing on his lips. "Did we get everything we needed, sweetheart?" he asked.

Calum licked his lips. "I think so."

"You *hope* so. I'm sure you'll remember something you missed once we're back home."

Calum chuckled nervously. "Probably."

The ex-boyfriend huffed, but Duane didn't care what he thought of any of this. Calum shouldn't care about it, either, and since he was so nervous, Duane stuck by him as the two of them went through checkout. They left the store together, and while Duane could still see the ex-boyfriend in the distance, the guy was climbing into his car, so he wouldn't be a problem for much longer. Still, Duane stayed close to Calum as he pushed his cart toward his car. He opened the trunk, and just then, the ex-boyfriend drove by.

Calum turned wide eyes toward Duane and leaned against him. Duane wasn't sure what he wanted or what he was willing to do, but he wrapped an arm around Calum's shoulders and pulled him even closer, pressing his nose against Calum's hair. He took a deep breath. Then, looking straight at the ex-boyfriend, he kissed the top of Calum's head.

The ex-boyfriend looked like he wanted to stop his car, climb out, and beat Duane into a pulp. Duane would have liked to see him try, but the asshole drove away without stopping.

Duane kept his arm around Calum's shoulders for a few seconds longer, then finally let go. "Everything all right?" he asked Calum.

To his surprise, Calum turned angry eyes at him. "What the fuck did you think you were doing?" he demanded to know.

If he'd been anyone else, Duane would have been offended. As it was, he couldn't think of anything that wasn't that Calum was adorable, even when he was pissed.

The gall of this guy. Calum didn't even know what to say. He might have been the one who started this, but he'd only wanted to show Rip that he could have someone in his life. Duane had fallen perfectly into that plan, acting like a loving boyfriend without missing a beat. He'd been sweet and gentle, and while Calum had been confused as to why he was going along with this, he'd also been grateful.

Then Duane had kissed him.

Okay, Calum had felt safe in Duane's arms, and he kind of wanted to push back into them. He didn't know Duane, though, and if he wasn't careful, he'd go from bad to worse. It wasn't something he was willing to risk, especially not after what happened with Rip.

Doing took a step back and raised both his hands. He'd hooked the small grocery bag in which they'd placed his purchases on his wrist, and it hung from there as he moved. "I apologize. I thought that was what you wanted since your ex was driving by."

Calum had seen Rip, but he hadn't expected a kiss. "There's no reason to make me feel like an idiot," he snapped. His heart was racing, and he had no idea how to deal with

Duane. He was grateful and should thank him, but part of him resisted—his asshole part.

"That's not what I was trying to do. I was just explaining why I did what I did, although, again, I apologize. I was surprised when you said I was your boyfriend, and I guess I got too deep into the part. Do you need help putting everything into your trunk?"

Calum stared. He'd expected Duane to storm off after berating him and snapping at him. It would have been his right to, especially after what he'd done for Calum. Instead, he was still there, smiling and looking like he was having the time of his life, even though they'd just left the grocery store.

"I can do it on my own," Calum said.

"I have no doubt you can, but since I'm here, I might as well help you."

He started moving bags, and Calum rushed to help. Did Duane think he was unable to do this? He'd said he didn't, but Calum had no idea what to think of him. Not many people would have gone along with what Calum had done, especially so smoothly. Even if they had, they'd have dumped Calum's ass at the grocery store door. Duane was still here, though, and it was confusing.

"I'm Duane, by the way," Duane said.

Calum turned to find him holding out a hand and glared at it. "I know. You introduced yourself to Rip."

"That's your ex?"

"Yeah."

Duane nodded. "I didn't like how he talked to you, so I'm glad you pulled me into the conversation. Do you need anything else?" He dropped his hand without Calum shaking it.

Who was this guy? Was he even real? Because he didn't feel like he was. "Why are you asking me that?" Calum didn't understand.

"I told you. I didn't appreciate how he talked to you, and

I've always had a protective streak. I guess it makes sense that I was hired to guard the forest."

Calum frowned. "You're one of the new guards?"

Duane nodded. "Yeah, so I'm new in town. I hope I didn't do anything I shouldn't have. Obviously, I've never met shifters before, and I'm trying my best not to be an asshole about it."

Calum gaped. "You're human."

Duane rubbed the back of his neck. "I am. You're a shifter."

"Everyone here is." Well, almost everyone. Josiah's boyfriend was human, as were the members of his team.

Duane nodded. "I'm not sure how to behave, but if you need anything else from me, feel free to call me." He reached into his pocket and took out the receipt from the grocery store and a pen.

Calum had never seen anyone carrying a pen around in their pocket, and he watched as Duane quickly wrote his number on the receipt, then handed it to him.

Should he take it? It was tempting, but he didn't know what to do with it. He doubted he'd ever call Duane.

Duane was gorgeous. He was way taller than Calum, taller even than Rip, which gave Calum a thrill. The fact that Duane's hair was bright red and that his pale skin was covered in freckles, along with his square jaw and wide smile, made Calum want to climb him like a tree, and he might be able to considering how tall Duane was. Duane's shoulders were broad, and his arms and thighs bulged with muscles. He looked like he could bench-press Calum without breaking a sweat.

He probably could.

Calum was hesitant as he reached for the receipt. If Rip had been in Duane's place, he'd have already yelled at Calum for not wanting him. He'd have thrown the receipt on the ground and stomped on it before leaving.

Why had Calum ever dated the asshole?

Calum couldn't remember the reason, and he didn't care. Duane couldn't have been any more different from Rip, and it was appealing. Calum was sure this would end in a disaster, but for once, he didn't care as he finally took the receipt from Duane's fingers.

Duane's smile widened. It wasn't just that he was built like a brick house and was so very clearly strong. There was a gentleness to him that Calum hadn't expected from a man like him, and even though he had to be annoyed at some of Calum's behavior, he hadn't said anything about it. He seemed to have infinite patience, which was something most people who dealt with Calum needed.

Everyone said so.

"I hope you'll call if you need anything," Duane said.

"I don't know." Calum wanted to be honest.

Thankfully, Duane didn't seem offended. Instead, he nodded. "Well, I just want you to know that you can. I won't get angry or anything." He hesitated. "And maybe you should stay away from your ex-boyfriend. He's an asshole."

Calum giggled and instantly slapped a hand against his mouth. He didn't *giggle*, for fuck's sake.

Duane seemed pleased, though, and he waved a hand at Calum as he walked away. Calum didn't miss the fact that Duane hadn't asked him for *his* phone number, and he wondered if that was on purpose. He didn't know anything about the guy, but he suspected that was true. Duane didn't want Calum to be afraid of him or to think that he was pushing his way into his life. He just wanted Calum to know that he wasn't alone, and while Calum already knew that, he was stunned to see it coming from a man he didn't know and a human to boot.

He had no clue what had just happened, but he pushed the receipt into his pocket, just in case. Even if he never used it, having someone care about him felt good. He might not understand why Duane cared, but he didn't think the why mattered. He was sure that if he called, Duane would answer and be right with him if he needed help. That was more than Calum could say of many people, including his old colony. He'd always been glad to be allowed to leave, but never as much as he was right now.

CHAPTER FOUR

Calum hung upside down from a branch. The darkness wrapped around him, and for the first time in weeks, he felt he was finally able to relax. Not entirely, since he was still thinking about Kaspar and Julian. He couldn't afford to be distracted when they were both about to give birth. Still, it was easier for him to forget about the two men for a few minutes when he was in his bat form, and shifting had reminded him that he wasn't doing it often enough. He felt he couldn't spare the time, but maybe that wasn't the case.

It was kind of ridiculous. He was a bat shifter, and everyone knew that. No one in the cete had ever had anything to say against that. The badgers didn't care that Calum was a bat, just like they didn't care that Julian was a weasel shifter and Kaspar a bear. *Calum* didn't like to be reminded of it, though. He wished he were a badger, too, so he could be a full member of the cete. As it was, he felt like Foley still had a say over what he said and did, and he didn't like that.

But Foley had no say in Calum's life, and he never would again. Thomas had made sure of that, and Calum would always be grateful.

He'd always be grateful for many things and many people.

But even though he lived with Kaspar and Julian to help them, sometimes being in the house could be a bit much. The two of them loved each other and were happy, and soon, they'd have a full family. No matter how much Calum cared about them and how much they cared about him, he'd always feel like he was an outsider, and he doubted anything would change that.

Sometimes, Calum just needed to get away from all the feelings. That was when turning into a bat and having an entire forest at his disposition came in handy. When he needed space, Calum shifted and left through his bedroom window. He hung around the trees for a while. Sometimes flew to Thomas's house or Kari's and watched them from his perch. It was probably a bit creepy, but it was good to remind himself that he had a family, even though he wasn't related to them by blood.

Calum stretched out his wings and took a moment to decide what he'd rather do. He could stay in his tree for a while longer, or he could fly off, maybe go home. But he, Julian, and Kaspar had agreed to take some time to themselves. Soon the babies would be born, and they wouldn't be able to do so. Calum hadn't wanted to leave tonight, but Julian had almost pushed him out the window, so Calum had given in.

He felt like he was always giving in to Julian and Kaspar. They didn't need his protection, but they did need his help, and it was good to feel useful and like he was giving something back to the cete who'd welcomed him with open arms.

Calum left his branch, but instead of heading home, he flew toward Thomas's house. He hadn't been out that long and didn't want to intrude on whatever Julian and Kaspar were doing. They needed time to be a couple before the babies came, and he wanted to give them that.

He flew under a branch between two trees and lowered as he reached Thomas's house. He wasn't sure where he wanted to perch, whether at the front of the house or at the back. Usually, at this hour of the night, Thomas and his wife were either having dinner or watching TV.

Calum wouldn't have known that if he hadn't been spying on half the cete for a while now. He realized he needed to stop, but it had helped him feel less alone, especially in the beginning. Sometimes it was almost as if he were eating and watching TV with the people he was spying on. He suspected Thomas would have welcomed him into his house and fed him while they watched movies together if he'd asked, but Calum never asked for anything. He couldn't let other people see he was vulnerable, especially when he was trying to be useful.

"It's incredible," a strong male voice said.

Calum almost lost his rhythm and just managed to avoid a tree trunk. He caught himself, but he was panicking and frantically attempting to find where the voice had come from.

He knew that voice.

"Well, I'm glad you're excited about this," Thomas said. "Hopefully, it will give you an incentive to protect us."

Duane made a small sound, almost as if he was disappointed in Thomas. "I don't need incentives. I'm here to do a job, and I knew what I was getting into before I signed up for it. You don't have to worry about me not doing my job."

"I won't deny that's good to hear. Unfortunately, some people who signed up to become guards haven't been what we're looking for."

"Were a lot of them here just to gawk at shifters?"

Thomas laughed.

Calum was headed straight toward them, and he needed to see if he was right. That was Duane he'd heard talking, right?

"I suspect they were. Thankfully, I had nothing to do with them. That's Luther's job."

"And he's good at it. I wouldn't worry about the people he actually hired. We're here for the right reasons."

There they were. Calum could see them, standing just a few feet from the porch steps of Thomas's house. They were facing each other, but he must have made a noise, because Duane suddenly turned. Calum was still flying toward him, and the panic was enough to make him feel breathless. He tried to turn as he opened his wings even wider, but it was too late. Duane's chest came closer and closer, and while Calum managed to steer, he still slammed face-first against it.

Ouch.

Just like Calum had suspected, Duane's chest was hard. It was like slamming against a brick wall, and he regretted it instantly. His entire face throbbed with pain, and as he slowly started sliding down Duane's chest, he found himself grateful for it. At least it was been enough to jerk him out of his panic, which meant he could fly away.

He tried opening his wings, but one of his claws was hooked into Duane's sweater. No matter how hard Calum pulled, he couldn't untangle it and could feel the panic rising again.

Then two massive warm hands wrapped around him.

Duane cupped his hands around the tiny bat that had slammed against him. He'd never had anything to do with bats, but he suspected that this wasn't their usual behavior. It made him wonder if maybe this bat was a shifter, but it was hard to wrap his mind around that possibility. How could an entire human being become something so tiny?

"Everything okay?" Thomas, the badger alpha, asked.

Duane gently extended one of the bat's wings and felt around. "I think so. Nothing feels broken, although I'm not an expert by any means."

"I don't think you need to be one. That might be a shifter you're holding."

Duane was aware of that, but would a shifter have slammed against him like this bat had? "Is there a way to know whether or not that's so?"

Thomas shook his head. "Not unless they decide to let you know."

Duane nodded. The bat was still pulling on his sweater with one of its claws, and Duane gently pulled it out. Just like a cat would have, the bad tried flying away as soon as it was free, and Duane opened his hands to allow it to do so. Whether it was a shifter or a real animal, he didn't want the bat to feel trapped.

He watched it fly away in the darkness until it disappeared. This new life of his was taking some time to get used to, but he'd expected it. He hadn't changed his mind about taking the job and didn't feel any different about being here. He was happy to be able to help, and so far, almost all the shifters he'd met had been good people. It was still amazing to think they could turn into animals, even though Duane had seen it happen several times now.

But more than that, it was amazing how welcoming everyone had been. He was here to talk to Thomas about possibly moving into badger territory, and he was tempted to say yes, even though he barely knew Thomas for now.

"I wouldn't be offended if I were you," Thomas said.

Duane blinked away from where the bat had disappeared. "I'm sorry?"

Thomas gestured. "About how they flew away. I don't know who they were, but I have a good idea, and if the bat was the person I think it was, I'm not surprised he ran away like that."

Duane grinned. "You mean he flew away."

"Either way, it has nothing to do with you."

"That's good. I don't want anyone to hate me, especially since I plan to stick around."

Thomas seemed pleased. "Are you?"

When he'd arrived, he'd invited Duane in, but Duane had asked if they could have this meeting outside. He'd spent a lot of time away from home, but being here brought him back to his childhood even though he'd never been there before.

He was used to the forest and the sounds that came from deep inside it, and he couldn't have picked a better place to settle down. He might have been hesitant in the beginning, but he wasn't anymore.

"As long as I'm allowed to, I'd love to stay in the forest," he told Thomas.

"And I'd love to have you with us. As I was telling you, our territory borders the human world. That means we're especially vulnerable to attacks coming from outside."

From what Duane had learned about the forest and the problems that had arisen recently, the badgers didn't have trouble dealing with other shifters. Humans were different, though, and not just because they couldn't turn into animals. Duane could only imagine what would happen if one of the shifters had to defend themselves from a human and ended up hurting or killing them. No matter what happened, a small part of the human population would be vocal about shifters being monsters and needing to be put down.

Duane wouldn't allow that to happen.

He wasn't the only one. He was working from the inside, but many people were outside doing the same. They wanted shifters to have equal rights, and Duane fully agreed, especially after meeting shifters. There was nothing different about them except for the fact that they could turn into animals. They had the same intelligence, the same abilities and capacities, and Duane was horrified that they'd been locked up in their forests for so long. They'd built nice lives here, with houses, towns, and grocery stores, but they deserved more.

Shifters deserved to be allowed to travel to visit family they might have in other forests. They should be allowed to go on vacation, see the ocean, and decide what they wanted to do with their lives. There was nothing Duane could do to help with that, but he could make sure no one in the forest got hurt by the humans protesting outside.

He'd seen them when he'd first arrived. Luther had emailed him every detail he'd need to get inside the forest, so he'd known to drive right up to the gates. Two guards had been there, and they'd looked wary until they'd realized who he was and why he was there. Then it had been easy to get details out of them, including the fact that a group of three humans had tried ramming through the gates the week before. They'd failed, but it wouldn't last forever, and when even one human managed to breach the forest, Duane and the other guards would need to be there.

"Has anyone tried getting into badger territory yet?" Duane asked.

"Not as far as I know, but as you'll find out soon, our territory is vast. It would be easy for a human to sneak in and hide. That's why we need guards, and a lot of them."

"I suppose you already have some kind of security."

"We do, just like every shifter group in the forest. Unfortunately, we're not trained to deal with humans, especially humans who are planning to antagonize us. That's where you and your people come in. If you take care of the borders, we can focus on the inside of the territory. We can make sure no other shifter gets any idea about invading us or taking us out."

From the way Thomas was talking, Duane felt like he might have had personal experience with those scenarios. He couldn't imagine it, but then he'd only just arrived.

"As I said, I'm open to moving in with the badgers. I just have a few questions, like where I'd stay."

"Well, I've been talking with Luther, and he mentioned that the long-term plan would be for you and your fellow guards to move to the forest permanently. Is that something you'd be interested in?"

Duane didn't even hesitate. "It is." He'd been thinking

about it, and even though it hadn't even been a week since he'd arrived, he already loved the forest and the people who lived here. He could see himself building a life here and had no problems with shifters. As far as he was concerned, this was the most perfect place in the world, and he was excited about possibly becoming a part of it permanently.

"Then I'm ready to offer you a house."

Duane hadn't expected that. "An entire house?"

"Well, if you're planning on sticking around, you might meet someone and build a family."

"I'm not planning on ever having children. It's not in the cards for me." Just the thought sent Duane into a panic.

"It can be a house on the smaller side, then."

"I don't want to be a bother to you or your people." He especially didn't want Thomas to offer him someone else's house.

But Thomas shook his head. "You're not. Our cete used to be much more numerous. We lost people over time, and we've been struggling with how expansive our territory is. It will be good to have someone live in one of the old houses again. Of course, they'll need some work, but I'm positive we can deal with that. In the meantime, you can stay where you are and settle in."

Duane couldn't help the smile that spread on his lips. Things were going even better than he'd expected them to — so much better that he could hardly believe it.

CHAPTER FIVE

Calum narrowed his eyes and watched Kaspar. Something was happening, and even though Kaspar hadn't said anything, Calum could see it. He briefly wondered if he should keep it to himself or ask Kaspar if he was okay, but he wasn't sure it was his business. Kaspar was an adult, and he was about to become a father. Surely, he should be able to keep things to himself if he wanted to.

But what if it was important? What if it was related to his children?

"How are you feeling?" Calum asked from the stove where he was cooking.

Kaspar had been walking in and out of the kitchen, and every time, he had a hand pressed against his lower back. He'd been hurting for several days now, but Cynthia had assured them it was because of the baby's weight.

Calum wasn't so sure that was true anymore.

Kaspar grimaced. "I'm fine."

"You don't look fine to me." Calum lowered the heat under the tomato sauce he was cooking. He wouldn't need to stick around, since it had to cook for a while, so he turned his focus on Kaspar. "What's going on?"

Kaspar leaned against the counter. "I don't know. My back hurts more than usual."

Calum slowly nodded. "Isn't that a sign of labor?"

"It is, but it's early. Julian is supposed to give birth before I do."

"That doesn't mean he will. Both of you are basically done

50

with your pregnancies. It's a matter of days now, and either one of you could give birth before the other." Maybe that was what was happening. "How long have you been in pain?"

"I told you. It's been a few days, but it's getting worse."

"Anything else hurts?"

Kaspar looked sheepish. "My lower stomach, but it only started a few hours ago."

"And you didn't tell me . . . why?"

"Because I didn't want to bother you."

"Kaspar, I'm here specifically so you can bother me. Now, why don't I take you upstairs to your bedroom? I'll call Cynthia as soon as you're comfortable."

"I don't think I can be comfortable ever again," Kaspar muttered, but Calum ignored him as he guided him toward the stairs.

They climbed slowly, and Kaspar had to stop once to lean against the wall. His expression was pained, and Calum suspected he was about to give birth. It might take him hours still, but Calum hoped not, for his sake.

Kaspar moved slowly, but they finally reached the bedroom he shared with Julian. Julian was sitting by the window looking outside, but when he heard them, he turned, smiling.

His smile became a frown when he saw Calum helping Kaspar inside. "What's going on?"

"I think he's in labor."

"I'm sure it's a mistake," Kaspar said with a groan.

Calum rolled his eyes. Sure, it was a mistake. "Just stretch out and try to rest, okay?"

Luckily, they'd been expecting this to happen, so the mattress was covered in a plastic sheet, and the sheets on their bed were old. They'd be able to throw everything away once Kaspar was done and the baby was here. They had more plastic and old sheets for Julian, but he wasn't who Calum needed to focus on right now.

"Can you stay with him?" he asked Julian.

"Of course. Call whoever you need to call."

The three of them had talked about this moment many times, so even though Calum could feel panic rising in his chest, he was able to focus. He knew exactly who to call, and he started doing so.

Cynthia was first. Calum explained what Kaspar had told him and that he'd put him to bed, and she promised she'd be there soon. She reassured Calum that even though Kaspar was supposed to give birth after Julian, it wasn't a surprise that he was first. The two of them had gotten pregnant so close that she'd been expecting something like this to happen. They were both at term, and the babies were perfectly fine the last time she'd checked a few days ago.

And one of them was ready to make his entrance into the world.

Next, Calum called Kari and Calder. Julian's son had declared he wanted to be here when his siblings were born, and both Julian and Kaspar had agreed. He wouldn't be in the bedroom with whoever was giving birth, but he'd be there to support them and in case they needed help. He and Calder weren't surprised and would be there as soon as they left Sebastian with Thomas.

The last on Calum's list was Thomas. He wasn't surprised to get his call, but he sounded delighted at the thought that one of the babies was about to come into the world. He loved babies, and Calum suspected he couldn't wait to meet the little guy.

Once Calum was done with his phone calls, he took a moment to breathe. He knew what to do. Cynthia had told him, and he'd gone over it enough times. He'd expected to be able to get through this without a worry, but now that it was happening, his heart was racing.

He couldn't help but wonder what would happen if

something went wrong, but he quickly shoved those thoughts away. It was the last thing he wanted to think about.

But even if everything went perfectly, he could still mess up. He was here to help Kaspar and Julian, which was what he needed to do and focus on. Cynthia would be the one taking care of Kaspar since she was the healer, which meant Calum's focus needed to be on Julian.

He could do that. He could do a lot of things if it meant taking care of the people he loved the most in the world.

So after taking one last deep breath, Calum headed toward the kitchen. He gathered several bottles of water and light snacks and carried everything to the bedroom, where he found Kaspar sitting on the edge of the bed, rocking slightly back and forth. Julian sat next to him, rubbing a hand against Kaspar's back.

Both of them looked up when they heard Calum, and Calum forced himself to smile at them. "I called everyone. Cynthia and Kari are on the way, so you don't have to worry about anything." He handed Julian one of the bottles, then another to Kaspar. "Remember to keep hydrated. Cynthia said it would help, and since you're still very much pregnant, Julian, you need to think of the baby."

Julian's smile was soft. "I am. I'm thinking of both the babies."

Calum swallowed. "I know you want to be here for Kaspar, and you will be, but if you need anything, please tell me. I won't be able to do much for Kaspar, but I can help you, and I'm planning on doing just that."

"Stop worrying. Both Kaspar and I trust you, and we know you'll do your best. Besides, I gave birth to Kari completely on my own in a shack in the woods. Kaspar and the baby will be fine, and I'm looking forward to meeting my second son."

Because Kaspar was having a boy, while Julian was having a girl. They were both delighted, as was everyone else. They deserved so much happiness, and Calum hoped they were getting it.

The next few hours were a whirlwind and, at the same time, slow. Calum didn't know where to focus. Cynthia arrived and focused on Kaspar while Kari and Calder took care of Julian. Kari and Calum took turns checking on him, which was a good thing, because while Kaspar had seemingly been in labor for several hours, he wasn't ready to give birth just yet. After three hours, Calum needed some air, so he left everyone in the house and stepped outside. He sucked in a breath, telling himself that everything was going well and that even though it was taking Kaspar a long time to have his baby, it didn't mean it was bad.

But it was about to happen. Calum had been waiting for this, and now, the moment had arrived, and he didn't know if he'd be able to do what he needed to do.

Duane was walking through the forest, getting familiar with cete territory. He'd walked past several houses, and while a few people had seemed wary of him, a wave and a smile had gone a long way. They knew he wouldn't be here if he wasn't trusted, which helped. Still, he couldn't wait until he truly was a part of the cete and people were comfortable with his presence.

And wasn't that odd to think?

It had been him, his father, and his brother all his life. He'd been close to some of the people he served with, but none of them had felt like family. The cete didn't feel like it yet, but Duane could see it wouldn't take long for that to happen. He felt more welcome here, with shifters surrounding him, than he ever had except for at home.

And he loved it.

He walked out of the forest to find himself in front of yet

another house. He started to turn to head back, but a voice stopped him.

"Are you following me?"

Duane frowned and turned to look at whoever had spoken. He thought he recognized the voice, and his eyes widened when he realized who it belonged to.

Calum stood on the porch, his hands on his hips, glaring at him. Duane was delighted about the expression on Calum's face—no one should be that adorable—and about the fact that he was with Calum again. When he'd given Calum his number, he hadn't expected the shifter to call him, and he'd been right. Calum hadn't, so maybe this was a way fate had found for them together again.

Duane strode toward the house. "Hi."

Calum narrowed his eyes. "So? Are you following me?"

"I'm not. I had no idea you lived here. Does that mean you're a badger shifter?"

Calum opened his mouth to answer, but a scream came from inside the house before he could.

Duane reacted on instinct, climbing the stairs and grabbing Calum to push him behind his back before reaching for the front door.

"What are you doing?" Calum snapped.

Duane turned to him. "You heard the scream, too."

"I did, and trust me, you don't want to go in there. Now answer me. Why are you here?"

Duane was confused. "Someone screamed, and you don't want me to go in?"

The second scream rattled his bones. Whoever the man screaming was, he was in extreme pain. If there was anything Duane could do for him, he wanted to do it, but it was clear Calum wouldn't allow him inside.

He rubbed his face, trying to find a way around it. "I already told you I was here to guard the forest. I'm planning on moving into badger territory."

Calum gaped. "Why didn't you tell me at the grocery store?"

"Because I didn't know about it yet. I've been staying with the other guards, but we've always known we'd be divided over the territories. The alpha here asked me if I wanted to move in permanently, and I said yes."

Calum stared at Duane with narrow, suspicious eyes. Duane supposed he'd be suspicious in Calum's place, too, but maybe he should be the one to feel that way. After all, someone in Calum's house was screaming his head off, and Calum didn't seem worried. He also didn't want Duane to go in, so maybe he was hiding something.

Was there a serial killer in the forest? Duane had no idea, but even if there was, he couldn't imagine Calum being that person. Still, he was way too calm considering the screaming happening upstairs.

Now that Duane was listening in, it wasn't the only thing he could hear. People were talking, and while he couldn't hear what they were saying, he was getting worried.

"I'm trained," he said.

"That's why you're a guard."

"I can defend you from whoever is hurting that person up there. I won't let anything happen to you."

For some reason, Calum seemed amused. "You don't have to defend me from anything, big guy. No one is hurting anyone beyond what's necessary right now."

"I don't understand."

The next scream made both of them jump. Calum moved toward the door, but Duane was in the way, and he wanted an explanation.

"Tell me what's happening. Maybe I can help."

"Not unless you're a healer. Kaspar is in labor, that's all."

Duane frowned. "Kaspar?" It was a weird name for a

woman, but Duane had heard stranger names.

"Yes. I live with him and Julian, and they're both pregnant. Well, Kaspar won't be for much longer. I need to go inside."

Duane's brain couldn't put the words Calum was saying together. "You're talking about this Kaspar person as if they're a male."

"That's because he is."

"How is he giving birth, then? Is he a trans guy?"

Calum stared at Duane for so long that Duane started shuffling his feet. Something was going on, and he hated not being in the know. He needed all the information he could find on every single situation he was in, dammit.

"No one told you about carriers," Calum eventually said.

"No, but I'm guessing it involves pregnancy and men?"

"It does. Carriers are cis male shifters who can become pregnant. That's what Kaspar and Julian are." He hesitated. "And what I am. Now, I really need to go."

Duane nodded, and Calum pushed past him and walked into the house, the door slamming behind him. Duane half wondered if he should go with him, but he felt numb from the news he'd just received.

He wasn't surprised shifters had hidden things from humans. He would have in their place, too. He also understood why they'd hidden the fact that some male shifters without a uterus could become pregnant and give birth.

He didn't blame them for any of that, but it would take a moment for his world to realign itself to include the news he'd just gotten. Here in the forest, some men had children they gave birth to, and Calum, the guy Duane had a crush on, was one of those men.

This wasn't something Duane had expected to happen when he'd gotten up this morning.

Calum stood just outside Kaspar's bedroom, looking in. Kari was behind him, but Calder had stayed downstairs, wanting to give Kaspar the privacy he needed. Calum supposed he should do the same. Kari was technically part of Kaspar's family, since Kaspar and his father were together, but Calum was nothing to Kaspar. He'd been there to help when Kaspar needed it, but surely he wouldn't want Calum to be in the room when his baby was born.

Kaspar screamed again, and following Cynthia's orders, pushed. Julian was sitting on a chair next to the bed, holding Kaspar's hand and softly talking to him. Calum couldn't avoid staring at his stomach. Soon it would be Julian's turn, and his position would be reversed with Kaspar's. Maybe then Calum would be taking care of this first baby. Maybe Kari would do it.

Calum had known things would change when the babies were born, but it had been easy to avoid thinking about that moment. Even though he'd seen Julian and Kaspar's stomachs grow and he'd known there were babies inside, he hadn't had the proof of it in front of his eyes.

He was about to get that proof. Julian and Kaspar were about to become a real family, and Calum had no idea whether or not he had a place in it.

"I'm going to get Calder. It's almost over," Kari murmured.

Calum nodded and looked away from Kaspar. He could still hear Cynthia, who stood between Kaspar's legs, telling him to push and how well he was doing. Calum agreed. Kaspar was in a lot of pain, even with the painkillers Cynthia had given him. Calum was glad he'd decided not to have children. This wasn't something he ever wanted to go through.

"One last push," Cynthia said, her voice soothing.

Kaspar grunted, and Calum had to look. Kaspar's face was flushed and he was sweating, but Julian didn't seem to care as he continued stroking his partner's arm.

"There you are," Cynthia murmured.

The next thing Calum heard was a baby crying. His knees went weak, and he had to hold himself up against the wall. A hand squeezed his shoulder, and he turned to look at Kari, who was once again standing beside him. His eyes glittered, and a wide smile curled his lips.

"I'm a big brother," he said.

Calum laughed. "You are. Congratulations."

They hugged, and at that moment, Calum felt like everything was all right in the world.

He, Kari, and Calder stayed outside while Cynthia took care of the baby. Calum had no idea what she was doing, but it didn't take long for her to put the baby in Kaspar's arms, then focus on the space between Kaspar's legs. Calum had no intention of watching that, and he briefly closed his eyes.

This was it. The first baby was born, and soon, the second would be here, too.

"You can come in," Kaspar said.

Kari pushed past Calum to be the first one in, and Calder went after him. Calum hesitated for a moment, though. Had Kaspar been talking to him? No matter what Kaspar always said about them being a family, Calum was never sure if that was the case.

"Calum?" Kaspar called out.

Calum sucked in a breath and opened his eyes. "You want me in there, too?"

"Of course."

Kaspar's cheeks were turning pale again, and he was obviously exhausted. Cynthia had covered his lower body, and while she was still working, it was easy to ignore her as Calum moved toward the upper part of the bed, where Kaspar was holding his baby. Julian leaned against Kaspar's side, and tears streamed down his cheeks as he looked down at his son.

They'd never looked so happy.

Kari and Calder were next to the bed on Julian's side. Calder had wrapped an arm around Kari's shoulders, and they were both beaming.

Calum realized that he was, too. Even with his doubts about them being a family or not and about belonging here, this was a joyous experience.

"So, what will you name him?" Cynthia asked.

Kaspar and Julian looked at each other. Their smiles were relaxed and happy.

Then Kaspar looked at Calum again. "His name is Cal," he said. "After Calum."

Calum's world stopped. Did this mean that Julian and Kaspar were naming their son after him? Why would they do that?

"That's a nice name," Cynthia said.

"Why?" Calum croaked.

Kaspar was still smiling. "Why not? You're the one person who has always been there for us. You supported us and stuck by our sides even when we're grumpy. You got up with us during the night and were there when we were throwing up in tandem. You've become family, and we wouldn't want it any other way."

Calum cleared his throat and prayed he wasn't about to cry. "I didn't expect this. Thank you." He didn't know what it would mean for him and the baby, but it didn't matter. Kaspar and Julian were showing him how much he mattered to them, something he'd doubted even though he had evidence to the contrary.

They loved him, and he loved them. Maybe they really were a family.

"Why don't you take him?" Kaspar asked.

Calum blinked. "Shouldn't Julian or Kari take him first?"

"I'm fine," Kari quickly said.

Calum looked at Julian.

Julian smiled. "I have years to hold him. Besides, I really need to go to the bathroom now that this is over."

Everyone in the room laughed. The baby made a snuffling sound, and Calum quickly went to check in on him. Considering how many people were here, it was superfluous, but Kaspar took advantage of that and handed him to Calum.

Calum took him and cradled him into his arms. His eyes burned more than before, and he knew he wouldn't be able to stop the tears from falling.

The baby looked like any other baby, but to Calum, he was special, and not just because he was named after him. He'd protect Cal and his sister with everything he had. The babies were part of his family, along with Kaspar and Julian, in a way Calum's parents had never been.

And he was never giving them up.

CHAPTER SIX

The sound of crying jerked Calum out of sleep. He blinked at his ceiling for a second. Then he remembered why he needed to get up.

Cal was crying.

Calum scrambled out of bed before Kaspar or Julian could do it. They both needed rest, Kaspar because he'd just given birth, and Julian because he was about to. Calum was taking up as much of the night feedings as he could, for which they were grateful, but sometimes he wondered if maybe he was doing too much. Cal was their child, not his, and he felt like he was intruding.

He walked into the nursery as he heard someone move in the bedroom Julian and Kaspar shared. Cal was crying in his crib, and Calum gently picked him up as Kaspar appeared at the door.

"He's hungry?" Kaspar asked in a whisper.

Calum nodded. "Sit down. I'll change him and hand him over."

"Let me go to the bathroom first."

Calum focused on the baby, and by the time Kaspar was back and sitting in the chair by the window, Cal was ready to eat. Calum handed him over, waited for a moment to be sure Kaspar and Cal didn't need anything else, then slunk out of the room.

He loved Cal as much as he loved Kaspar and Julian. He'd been the one who offered to help with the babies in the beginning, and they'd agreed. They'd have allowed him to live with them even if he hadn't, but he felt he owed them this. Sometimes, though, it was hard. Calum felt a bit like an intruder who didn't have a place in this family, and he wasn't sure how to get over that or even if he could. He was doing everything to help, but was it enough? Should he ask Thomas to find him another place to stay?

Calum went back to bed, but it took him a long time to fall asleep again. The next time he woke up, the sun was streaming through his window, and he blinked, wondering what time it was. Since Cal had been born, Calum had lost all sense of time and didn't have routines anymore. He just got up when he had to take care of Cal and his fathers and worked around the house. It didn't matter if he got up at eight rather than ten or eleven. No one cared, least of all Julian and Kaspar, who were exhausted.

Calum's phone vibrated on his nightstand, and he picked it up, wondering who it was. He frowned when he saw Thomas's name on the screen. The alpha didn't usually call him. They didn't have much to talk about, especially not now that Calum was staying out of trouble. Maybe he wanted to know how Cal was and didn't want to bother Kaspar or Julian to find out.

Calum propped himself on his pillows as he answered. "Thomas," he said.

"Good morning. I didn't wake you, did I?"

"No, don't worry."

"I remember how it was when my sons were born. In the beginning, it feels like you're standing out of time. It gets easier, though."

Calum didn't doubt that, but Cal was only a few days old. It would take them some time to get used to having him in the house, and he suspected that Julian would give birth by the time they had, and they'd have to get used to it all over again.

"They're lucky to have you," Thomas continued. "I know

my wife wished she could have had someone living with us and helping her with the baby, and we only had one at a time."

"You still had other kids to take care of, even though they weren't all newborns," Calum pointed out.

"That we did. Anyway, I was wondering if you could come to my office."

That gave Calum pause. He trusted Thomas, but something in his tone told Calum something was going on. "When?"

"Right now, if you can."

Calum briefly lowered the phone and listened to the house. It was silent, which probably meant everyone was still sleeping. He raised the phone again, wishing he could say no but knowing better. He wouldn't find out what was happening until he talked to Thomas, and he might as well get it out of the way as soon as possible. "I think everyone is still asleep, so it shouldn't be a problem. Give me about half an hour."

"Take all the time you need."

The sound of someone protesting reached Calum's ear, but Thomas had already hung up. Calum stared at his phone for a moment, his thoughts twirling. Thomas wasn't about to kick him out of the cete. That was one thing Calum was sure of. Even if the alpha tried, Calum had many people who cared about him and wouldn't take it nicely.

So Calum wasn't going anywhere. That still didn't explain what Thomas wanted from him. Calum hadn't done anything that would warrant his alpha calling him to his office.

Still, since he'd said yes, he got out of bed, quickly showered, and dressed. When he got to the kitchen, he found Kaspar standing there, leaning against the counter and staring out the window. For a moment, he thought Kaspar had fallen asleep like that, but Kaspar turned and smiled at him.

"Good morning," he said.

"How are you feeling?" Calum asked as he poured himself a cup of coffee.

"Still achy, but I'll be fine."

Kaspar would be, and so would Julian. Calum couldn't deal with anything else. "Good. Thomas called and said he wanted to see me, so I'm headed out. Do you need me to do or get anything before coming back?"

"I think we have everything we need, but thank you. And please, stay out for as long as you need. You don't have to rush back home just because of us."

"Maybe I want to rush back home because I want to spend time with you guys."

"I hope that's the reason. You've been spending most of your time here." Kaspar hesitated. "As much as I enjoy your company, sometimes, I wonder if we're stifling you."

"If anything, I'm stifling myself. Don't worry about me needing people. For now, I don't want to meet anyone, and I'm fine with my life how it is." Maybe once the babies were a bit older, Calum would move out, or at the very least give himself a chance to meet people. He was only twenty-one, and while he didn't want a relationship right now, that would no doubt change. He was young, though, and he had time to find someone he liked and who treated him right.

"Let us know if there's anything we can do," Kaspar said as Calum left.

"You know what you can do? Go back to bed and get more sleep. Cal will be awake soon, and you'll need all your energy when that happens."

Kaspar's chuckle followed Calum to the door. The air was cold when Calum opened it, but he liked it. It was a stark difference from inside the house and helped clear his thoughts.

He walked briskly, taking the path that would lead him to Thomas's house. He passed a few badgers in their animal form and nodded at them, but he didn't stop. Besides, beyond leaning down and sniffing them, there was no way for him to recognize them.

All in all, it had taken him just under half an hour to reach Thomas's house. He stomped his feet as he climbed the porch steps and raised his hand to knock, and he was still wondering what was happening when the door swung open.

Alex, Thomas's son and the future alpha, looked worried. That was enough to raise Calum's hackles.

"What is it?" he asked, hoping Alex would tell him.

Alex opened his mouth, possibly to finally explain, when two men appeared in the entrance. There was Thomas, who Calum had come to see, but he wasn't alone, and it took a second for Calum to recognize the other.

Foley.

Calum sucked in a breath. What was his old alpha doing here? There was no doubt Calum was involved in whatever Foley was planning, but Calum had no intention of giving him the satisfaction. He turned around and rushed off the porch and away from the house, ignoring the men calling out for him to come back.

He was never going back. He didn't care what Foley wanted or why he was here. Badger territory was Calum's home now, and he'd do anything he could to stay, even shifting and staying in his bat form to live in the forest.

He'd rather do that than go back to the bats.

Duane was hanging out with another guard, Saul, when they heard the yelling. They looked at each other, and Duane wondered if whatever was happening was their business. Probably not, but he couldn't stay away if someone was in trouble, and he suspected the same went for his new friend.

He and Saul had been exploring badger territory. Saul was another one of the guards Thomas had talked to and offered a permanent place in his territory, and while he was still thinking about whether or not he'd move here, he'd been spending a lot of time with the badgers. That was enough to make Duane wonder if deep inside, Saul had already made his decision, but it was none of his business, so he hadn't brought it up.

"We should probably check that out," he said as he moved toward the yelling. Unless he was wrong, it had come from Thomas's house, which was kind of worrying. He and the other guards were only supposed to guard the borders, with the badgers taking care of security inside badger territory, but maybe they could use some help. Even if they didn't want him to be involved, Duane couldn't just hang back until he was sure no one was in danger.

"I don't know. We're not supposed to intervene in this kind of situation."

"We don't know what the situation is," Duane pointed out. He didn't miss that Saul followed him even as he protested.

"I suppose we can see what's happening, at the very least," Saul agreed.

Duane was glad they'd decided to check things out once they reached Thomas's house. He had no idea what was happening, but Calum was in front of the house, trying to pull away from a guy holding his arm. Thomas and his son Alex stood around them, and they didn't look happy. Thomas was harshly talking to the guy holding Calum, but the guy didn't seem to be about to let go of Duane's fake boyfriend.

Saul and Duane looked at each other. Saul was more hesitant, but Duane strode toward the little group, eager to help Calum. Even though they weren't actually together, he felt some kind of responsibility when it came to the man. He'd been there to help Calum when he needed him, and he seemed to be in a similar situation now.

"I have rights over him," the asshole was saying.

"You don't, just like I don't," Thomas answered.

Duane suspected he was having a hard time staying patient. He'd never seen Thomas angry before, but it was a sight to behold. Duane suspected that the asshole had to be important, because otherwise, Thomas wouldn't have hesitated to kick him out without trying to explain.

"He's a carrier," the asshole snapped. "More than that, he's a bat shifter. He belongs with the colony, not with the badgers."

"He's not the only non-badger shifter we have here. They all belong with the cete as much as they decide."

"That's your way to do things, but not mine. Calum is a bat, and as such, he belongs with the colony, which is where he'll go once this conversation is over." The guy straightened his back. "And it is."

Duane hesitated. This sounded like cete trouble, which in theory, he shouldn't be involved in. Before he could decide whether or not to turn around and leave, Calum raised his head, and their gazes met. Calum's eyes widened, and, to Duane's surprise, he threw himself forward.

It was enough to startle the asshole holding him. Duane saw the man's hand tighten, and Calum didn't get free, but he got close enough to Duane to wrap his arms around one of Duane's and hold on tightly.

"Help me," he begged.

Duane had no idea how he could help Calum, but it didn't matter. He'd do whatever he could.

Duane looked at the asshole holding Calum. "You should let go of him."

The man's eyes narrowed. "Who are you to talk to me like that? Do you know who I am?"

"From where I stand, you're an asshole."

The man made a strangled sound. Calum pulled his arm away from him again, and this time, the man let go, possibly because he was startled by the way Duane was talking to him.

"How dare you!" The man stepped forward and tried to catch Calum's arm again.

Duane grabbed Calum and pushed him behind himself. Then he stood in front of him, ready to protect him. "He doesn't want to go with you. I don't care who you are and what you want from him. He's an adult, and he can make his own decisions."

"He's a carrier." The last word dripped with disgust. "Until recently, they weren't allowed to make their own decisions."

That was something Duane was still looking into. After Calum had explained about his friend giving birth, Duane had talked to Thomas, who'd told him what had been happening. He'd given Duane details about how the carriers had been treated in the forest and how things had changed for them recently. He hadn't hidden the fact that some people believed carriers should still be treated like they were nothing more than incubators, which Duane found revolting.

"But we are now," Calum said from behind Duane's back. He put a hand on Duane's hip and leaned around him to look at the asshole. "And my decision is to stay here with the badgers. I'm never coming back to the colony. It's not my home anymore, and you're not my alpha. Thomas is."

The asshole—apparently Calum's old alpha—tightened his hands into fists. He looked like he might be about to hit Calum, but he'd have to go through Duane to do that.

And Duane wouldn't allow him to take even one more step toward Calum.

"Don't you dare talk to me that way," the asshole snapped.

"He'll talk to you any way he wants," Thomas said. "You heard him, Ralph. He's chosen his home, and it's here, not with your colony. You won't convince him otherwise, and I won't allow you to drag him away from his home. My son will walk you back to your car and make sure you leave our territory."

Ralph looked at Calum again. "You'll regret this."

"I haven't yet, and I never will." Calum swallowed so loudly that Duane could hear him. "I have everything I've ever wanted here. I have friends and my boyfriend, and we're planning a life together."

Duane's eyes widened, but he didn't say anything to contradict Calum. He also didn't say anything when Calum walked around him and wrapped an arm around his waist. His instinct was to wrap his own arm around Calum's shoulders, and as he did so, they both stared Ralph down.

The alpha frowned. "He's human."

"So?" Calum asked with a shrug. "He's treated me better than Rip ever did."

"At least Rip is a bat shifter."

"He could be a golden goose shifter, and I wouldn't care. I'm with Duane, and he's everything I ever wanted."

Duane had no doubt he was miles better than Calum's ex-boyfriend after meeting the guy, but everything Calum ever wanted? He supposed that as long as Calum didn't want much, he could be that for him, but maybe he and Calum should have a talk about Duane being his fake boyfriend. This was the second time it had happened, and Duane couldn't help but wonder if it would happen again. He wasn't sure how he felt about the possibility that it would—or that it wouldn't.

What he was sure of was that he wanted Calum to be comfortable and happy, and apparently, acting as his fake boyfriend when he needed him would make that happen. Duane might be an idiot for giving in again, but he didn't care.

So he held Ralph's gaze, grinned, and kissed the top of Calum's head.

Calum did his best not to look at Thomas and Alex. They had to know he was lying, but he didn't care. Foley would believe them. Rip had, after all, and Calum would tell them about their encounter at the grocery store if he had to.

Calum was relieved Duane was going along with this again. He hadn't treated him right, and while he might not admit it to Duane himself, he could admit it to himself. If he got out of this without having to leave the badgers, he'd have to thank Duane, at the very least.

But it was early for that. Foley was still staring at him as if he was trying to find a way to convince Calum to come along. He wouldn't be able to drag Calum away by force, because Thomas, Alex, and Duane wouldn't allow him to. He wasn't going to give up, though. Calum knew his old alpha, and he was sure of that. That meant he'd have to be sneaky, and while it wasn't the way Foley usually did things, he was clearly desperate to get his hands back on Calum.

Why? None of this made sense. Foley had brought Calum to the badgers, although that had been back when carriers were in danger of being taken by the council. As soon as the laws had been changed and it had been safe for carriers to go home, Foley had appeared to take Calum back to the colony. He'd been stunned when Calum had told him he wasn't going anywhere, but he'd left easily enough. Calum had thought he'd washed his hands of him and that he'd leave him alone, but clearly, he'd been wrong.

So very wrong, and he suspected he knew what was happening. He just couldn't accept it.

"Rip isn't the reason I'm here. There are plenty of other bat shifters who would be happy to date you," Foley said.

He looked like he was trying to smile to reassure Calum, but instead, he was freaking Calum out. "I don't need to date a bat shifter. I have Duane."

"He's human. He doesn't understand you like a shifter

71

would, and he doesn't understand what you need." Foley looked Duane up and down. "He should never have been allowed in the forest."

Calum wasn't surprised Foley thought that way. Calum wasn't an alpha or part of the council, yet he understood why humans had been allowed in the forest and were being used as guards. Surely Foley had to see it made sense.

But even if he didn't, it wasn't Calum's business. He hadn't been part of the colony in months and wasn't going back, no matter what Foley was saying or plotting.

"Well, even though he's human, Duane has never treated me like I'm a freak of nature. He's never tried to use me in any way, least of all to have a child when he knows there's nothing I want less in the world."

"No one is planning on forcing you to do anything."

But Calum didn't believe his old alpha. Why was Foley trying so hard to take him home if not to push him into something he didn't want? Hell, trying to get him to go home was pushing him into something he didn't want. Even if Calum had trusted Foley before, he wouldn't trust him anymore after this conversation.

"Aren't you trying to force him to go with you?" Duane asked.

Foley bared his teeth at him, and while they were human teeth, it still sent a shiver down Calum's spine.

"That's it," Thomas snapped. "Calum isn't going anywhere, not even back to the colony."

Foley finally turned his attention to him. "You'll change your mind. He's nothing but trouble."

"I'm not the one who needs to change his mind. Calum is the only one who can decide where he wants or doesn't want to go."

"And even if Thomas doesn't want me here anymore, I won't come back to the colony," Calum said. "The colony never felt like home, and I have nothing to go back to."

Foley looked like he wanted to hit something, preferably Calum, but he finally gave up after Alex stepped closer to him. "This isn't over," he said.

As far as Calum was concerned, it was, and he was relieved when Alex guided Foley back to his car. Calum should have recognized the cart when he'd first arrived, but he hadn't even thought about the possibility of Foley being here to talk to Thomas, least of all about him.

They all watched Foley climb into his car and drive off. Once he was out of sight, Alex joined them, and Calum wasn't sure where to look. He owed Thomas and the others an explanation about why he so fiercely didn't want to go back to the colony.

He wasn't looking forward to it.

Now that the asshole had left, Duane looked back to see Saul hovering at the edge of the forest. He'd been there to help, but they hadn't needed him to step in. He raised a hand to wave at Duane, and Duane waved back. They'd see each other back in the house they shared with the other guards, and Duane had no doubt Saul would ask him what had happened.

He wasn't sure how to answer that question.

From what he'd understood, the asshole had been Calum's old alpha and was trying to take him back to their bat colony. The problem was that Calum had no intention of going with him, and the guy couldn't take no for an answer. Thankfully, Calum hadn't faced him alone, but Duane couldn't help but wonder what would've happened if, instead of his ex-boy-friend, Calum had met his alpha at the grocery store. Would the guy have tried to drag him back to the colony?

"I hate to ask you this, but I think we should talk," Thomas said.

Calum was rigid with tension, but he was still in Duane's arms. He nodded curtly, and even though Duane didn't want to let go, he dropped his arm. Calum blinked and frowned, then his eyes widened, and he took a step away from Duane.

"Thank you," he murmured.

"You don't have to thank me, but I'd appreciate it if you could give me an explanation. This is the second time I've played your boyfriend."

Calum frowned. "No one forced you to do it."

"No, and I'll do it again even if you don't give me an explanation, but even so, I'd like to know what I'm up against." Duane suspected that Calum's old alpha wouldn't give up. Whatever the guy wanted from Calum, it had been enough to bring him all the way here and threaten Calum in front of another alpha.

"Why don't we go inside?" Thomas offered. "If Calum is comfortable with it, Duane could come with us. I don't fully understand what's happening, but he stepped in to help, and I suspect it's not the first time he's done so."

Calum sighed. "It's not. He played my boyfriend when I saw my ex at the grocery store."

Thomas nodded but didn't ask to know more. He seemed satisfied with the explanation.

They followed Thomas into the house. Duane wasn't surprised when they went straight to the office. They sat, Calum taking the chair in the middle. He seemed uncomfortable, and while Duane understood, if they truly wanted to help Calum, they needed to know what was going on.

"I don't mind being your fake boyfriend," he said since Calum wasn't talking.

He seemed to be gathering his courage, and Duane wondered what was so horrible that he'd need to behave that way.

"You don't know what you'd be up against," Calum murmured.

"Is it your entire colony?" Thomas asked. "Or Foley in particular? He wants you to go back, and I feel he has a good reason for that. It's clearly a reason you don't agree with."

"I'm not sure why he's so eager to get me back, although I suspect part of it is that he was arranging a marriage for me before he had to bring me here," Calum slowly explained.

Duane frowned. In any other situation, he wouldn't have thought it possible for people to be forced into arranged marriages these days, but clearly, he was wrong. It probably had to do with the fact that Calum was a carrier, and while that hadn't changed, the laws had. Calum didn't have to get married to anyone he didn't want.

Duane suspected Calum's old alpha didn't care about that.

Thomas sighed. "I see. Unfortunately, I can't say I'm surprised. You should stay as far away from Foley as you can."

"That's what I've been trying to do." Calum got to his feet. "But he's everywhere. I saw him at the grocery store and then here. How am I supposed to avoid him when he comes to my home? It feels like he knows exactly where I'm going and where I'll be most vulnerable, and I hate it."

There was pain in Calum's voice, which made Duane believe there was more to the situation than a possible arranged marriage. Calum was still hiding something, and while Duane was curious, he wasn't about to ask what that something was. Calum deserved his privacy, and clearly, whatever had happened to him, it was still painful.

Duane sighed. He'd already liked Calum before, and not only because he was cute as a button. Everything in Calum triggered Duane's instinct to protect, and Duane wanted him to know that he was here if he needed help.

"Well, whatever this Foley guy is planning, you can always count on me," he said. "I'll be your fake boyfriend anytime you need me to be."

Calum turned wide eyes at him. "Why would you do

that?"

"Why not? You need protecting, and protection is why I'm here."

Calum opened his mouth, but nothing came out. He closed it again, shook his head, then rushed toward the door.

Duane started to get up, but a hand on his shoulder stopped him. Alex shook his head, and Duane was forced to let Calum go.

"He needs time," Thomas said.

"I don't have a problem with that. I just want to help him."

"That's what we've been trying to do since he arrived, but he's been hiding so many things. I understand why, and I don't blame him, but we need to know everything to help. Maybe you'll manage to get answers out of him."

"I can try, but I'm not making promises." Because Duane wasn't actually Calum's boyfriend. He was a stranger, and while Calum might be more inclined to tell him his story because of that, the opposite could also be possible.

"I don't need you to make promises," Thomas said. "I don't even need you to protect Calum. It's not part of your job."

"Maybe not, but he's a member of your cete, and eventually, I hope this place will become my home. That means he'll be a member of my family as much as he is of yours right now. If there's anything I can do to help him, I'll do it." Duane could deal with sleazy alphas. What he couldn't deal with was Calum being hurt.

CHAPTER SEVEN

Duane had been giving Calum time and space, but Calum still hadn't come to him. As far as he knew, Calum had barely left the house he lived in with his friends, which was starting to worry him.

He didn't like it. Calum had every right to leave his house and go to the grocery store or do whatever else he wanted. He shouldn't have to fear someone would take him or hurt him, and the thought that he was made Duane angry.

The trouble was that without knowing what the problem was, there wasn't much he could do.

It was frustrating and distracting. Thankfully, so far, no human had tried jumping the fences while Duane was working, but he knew himself well enough to realize that if someone tried and he was distracted, it wouldn't be good. He needed to do something, and the only person he could think to talk to was Thomas. So after his shift was over, he headed toward the alpha's house.

He didn't fully understand shifter hierarchy yet, but Thomas was the leader, and he could tell he was good at it. Thomas was gentle and just a nice guy all around, but when he needed to be, he could also be fierce. Duane had seen hints of that when Thomas had dealt with Foley, and he had no doubt that Thomas would do whatever he could to keep Calum safe. He'd told Duane to give Calum space and time, but for some reason, Duane felt like they were running out of time.

Foley had his reasons to come over and try to get Calum

back. They had to be important, and while Duane wasn't sure if an arranged marriage was important enough, it wouldn't surprise him. What if the guy Calum had been supposed to marry was holding something over Foley's head?

Duane didn't care about the reason, though. He just cared that it might make Foley desperate, which in turn would push him to do something stupid. If he couldn't get to Calum outside of badger territory, he might try to sneak in and grab him here, and that could push the colony and the cete into a war.

None of this was Duane's business. He was human, and he'd been brought in to patrol the borders, not to deal with this kind of internal politics. The problem was that Calum was right in the middle of it, and Duane couldn't ignore that. He wanted to protect Calum, but once again, he was back to his initial problem.

He didn't know Foley well enough to do so.

When he knocked on the door, Thomas answered. He smiled and waved Duane in, but instead of going to his office, he led Duane to the kitchen.

"I don't know about you, but I could do with a cup of coffee," Thomas said.

"I won't say no. I was up early this morning."

Thomas nodded. "Morning shift?"

"I'll be glad when the shifts change." And they would. Luther was still talking to people and vetting them, so hopefully, they'd have more guards soon.

They sat at the kitchen table. The place smelled of coffee and cookies, reminding Duane of his mother. She'd always loved to bake, even though often the results had been disasters. It had never mattered, though. Duane, Sheridan, and their father had always eaten whatever she prepared, even when it tasted foul. Duane doubted that what Thomas's wife baked was bad, though.

The room was homey, with yellow curtains at the window

and bad drawings and pictures on the fridge. Duane didn't know every cete member yet, but he recognized Thomas's sons with their children. It made him ache for home, even though he already loved living in the forest.

"So, what can I do for you?" Thomas asked.

Duane was thankful for the distraction. "I've been thinking about Calum's problem with his old alpha."

Thomas wrapped his hands around his cup and nodded. "I've been thinking about Calum, too."

"Has he told you anything more?"

"Unfortunately, no. I've barely seen him, and when I reached out to the men he lives with, they told me he hasn't been leaving the house. Kaspar went to the grocery store the other day, even though he gave birth last week."

"So you don't know anything more than what he told us."

"I wish I did. It's clear Foley is planning something, and I don't know how to help Calum. It's not a bad thing that he's been staying home, because it means he's more protected, but it's not the life I want him to live. He and the other carriers are finally free to do whatever they want. It's not right that he needs to hide."

"I agree. I want to help him, too."

"I was surprised when he latched onto you the way he did. The two of you already knew each other?"

"Not exactly. When I first arrived, I heard him talking to his ex-boyfriend at the grocery store, and it wasn't going well. I acted as if I were his boyfriend, and it worked. I guess he decided to do the same."

"It was certainly enough to get Foley to back off." Thomas's gaze was calculating.

Duane couldn't tell what the alpha was thinking, but as long as it meant Calum was safe, he'd go along with whatever plan Thomas was cooking up. "Would thinking Calum is with me be enough to stop whatever arranged marriage Calum was talking about?"

Thomas leaned back. "I'm not sure. Before, I'd have said no, especially since you're human. It wouldn't have mattered, though. Carriers were nothing more than objects to move around and force into things, and Foley would have done that if Calum didn't do what he wanted. Now, if he forces Calum into anything he doesn't want, he'd have to deal with the council, but that's only if someone finds out. If he locks Calum up and doesn't allow him to talk to anyone, there would be no way for people to find out what's being done to him, least of all the council."

"His friends would notice something is wrong with him."

"Maybe so, but it's not that easy. We do have a team that focuses on rescuing carriers, and they might be able to sneak in, but the individual territories aren't open. I couldn't waltz in as if it was Northwood, for example. Our territories aren't neutral. We're particular about the people we allow in, and if Foley is doing something he shouldn't be doing, it's going to be even harder to get into bat territory."

"But he came right in the other day."

"He did, and he's aware that I wasn't happy about it. As an alpha, though, I gave him the respect he deserved, or at least, the respect I thought he deserved. I allowed him to come in and talk to Calum, and I wish I hadn't."

"We need to know him better and find out what he's planning."

"How are you going to do that?"

There was only one person who could answer their questions. "We need to talk to Calum again."

Thomas grimaced. "I thought you'd say that. I can't say I'm looking forward to it."

"Calum is grumpy."

"That he is, but that's not why I wish I didn't want to talk to him. Whatever happened to him when he lived with the colony, he's never told anyone, as far as I'm aware. I don't know if they abused him, and I don't want to bring up bad memories if I can avoid it."

Duane agreed, but unfortunately, he didn't think they could avoid it.

"But you're right," Thomas continued. "We need to talk to Calum, and soon. I don't want to be surprised by Foley's next move. Calum is part of the cete, which means it's my job to protect him."

"Technically, it's not mine, but I'm willing to do whatever it takes."

Thomas stared at Duane for a moment. "That's good to know. Maybe you're already becoming part of the cete."

Maybe Duane was, or maybe he just wanted to help Calum. He knew himself, though. It was more than Calum's vulnerability that appealed to him. It was Calum himself, and Duane wouldn't say no to the opportunity of spending more time with him. He just wished he didn't have to do so while also keeping Calum safe from his asshole ex-alpha.

Calum wasn't surprised when Thomas called him. He hadn't seen the alpha since the day Foley had come to badger territory, and it was on purpose. He'd been avoiding Thomas, knowing he'd have to answer questions he didn't want to answer the next time he saw him.

And apparently, it was that time.

"When do you need me to come?" Calum asked when he answered.

"Whenever you can. Right now would be great, since I have Duane in my office."

He was another person Calum had been avoiding. Today was going to be a disaster, wasn't it? "Why is he there?"

"We were talking about your situation and what we can do

to protect you. We can talk about it on the phone, but I'd be more comfortable if you were in front of me."

"Because if I am, you'll ask me questions about why I never wanted to go back to the colony."

"I won't deny I feel we need to know more about Foley. I always thought he was on the right side of things. He fought with us against the people who wanted to keep carriers under their thumbs. What he's doing now doesn't make sense."

Calum almost laughed. He had no doubt Foley had worked with Thomas. What he doubted were Foley's reasons to do so.

His old alpha wasn't an idiot. He'd seen the way the wind blew and had chosen the winning side, but that didn't mean he agreed with what they wanted. But it wasn't just a carrier thing. Foley liked control, and he wanted it to be absolute. He hadn't liked that the council wanted to control his people, even if it was only the carriers. Calum was still young, but he wasn't the first carrier to be born into the colony. A few had been taken away by the council after they turned twenty-six and handed over to whoever paid more money for them. Foley had been pissed, and he'd made sure it wouldn't happen with Calum.

That didn't mean he wasn't planning on using Calum himself.

Calum sighed. Thomas deserved answers, especially if the badgers were about to end up in a war with the bats. Calum hoped that wouldn't happen, but he wouldn't put anything past Foley, including war.

"I'll come," he said.

"Good. We'll be waiting for you."

Even though it was the last thing Calum wanted to do, he'd known he wouldn't be able to avoid this conversation forever. So, after hanging up, checking on Kaspar and Julian and the baby, and changing clothes, he headed out.

It took him more time to reach Thomas's house this time. He was dragging his feet, but it wasn't like Thomas was going to forget he was supposed to go there. He was waiting for him, and sure enough, Calum barely had the time to knock on Thomas's door when it opened, revealing the alpha himself.

Thomas's smile was gentle and kind. "Come in. It's getting cold out there."

"Well, it's winter."

"Which is why I avoid going out as much as possible." Thomas visibly shuddered. "I've never liked the cold."

Calum found himself smiling. Thomas was being ridiculous, but he was probably trying to get Calum to relax. It would take more than that, but it was a start.

After leaving his jacket at the entrance, Calum followed Thomas to his office. Since Thomas had told him Duane was there, he wasn't surprised to see him sitting in one of the chairs. What did surprise him was that Duane got to his feet to welcome him. He wasn't a damsel in distress, dammit.

"It's good to see you," Duane murmured as he sat back down.

Even with everything else, it *was* a pleasure to see him again. Calum wasn't sure what to make of it or why he felt that way. It was probably because Duane had made him feel protected and wanted at the grocery store, and Calum was having a hard time moving away from that.

Thomas sat behind his desk and leaned forward. "I understand that talking about whatever happened isn't going to be easy for you," he said slowly. "I've heard many stories about how the carriers were treated by their alphas, and if I didn't feel this was important, I wouldn't push you to tell us what happened. I'm honestly just trying to understand and guess what Foley's next move will be. He had balls, coming into our territory and trying to drag you away. I didn't expect something like that from him, and I want to be prepared next time."

Calum swallowed as he nodded. "I understand. But I don't know what he's planning. I was never privy to any kind of information when it came to leading the colony or its relationship with other shifter groups."

"Because you're a carrier?"

"Because Foley doesn't talk to anyone about this kind of thing, except for his beta and his heir. He believes it's worthless for anyone else to know what's going on. I always thought he liked keeping us in the dark because it meant he had better control over us."

Thomas sucked in a breath. "He craves control."

Calum nodded curtly and stared down at his hands. He didn't know where to start, but the beginning would be good.

"He's always been like that. He became alpha when I was a kid, so my life has always been like this. He views everyone, including other bat shifters, as inferior. He wants full control and power, which is why he keeps us unaware of what's going on around us. We had no idea what was happening with the carriers until he grabbed me and brought me here. I didn't even know where we were going or why until I arrived and one of the other carriers told me about it."

"I can only imagine how terrifying it was for you."

Thomas understood. He might never have been in Calum's situation, but that didn't mean he couldn't put himself in his place. "I didn't know you or anyone else at the Bishop house. I didn't know what you'd do to me, and I tried protecting myself by pushing everyone away. Even after I realized that you weren't going to harm me, it was easier, because I didn't want to lose everything. I knew Foley would come back for me, and he did."

"But you refused to go with him."

"Because you'd given me an alternative. When I first got here, I didn't think that would be so. As soon as you said it, I realized how much my life could change, and I knew what I had to do."

"What about the arranged marriage?" Duane asked.

Calum carefully avoided looking at him. He wanted Duane to like him, even though he didn't understand why. The last thing he wanted was to see pity in Duane's own eyes. He wouldn't be able to stand it.

"That's more control," Thomas said.

Calum nodded. "My parents informed him when they realized I was a carrier, but it was one more thing he kept to himself. I started dating Rip, and while Foley wasn't happy about it, he also didn't forbid us to be together. I'm still surprised, to be honest."

"I'm not. He was giving you a hint of freedom to control you better. In your eyes, he was the one person who could give you good things and take them away. That would have pushed you to go along with what he wanted."

That made sense. Calum hated it, but he couldn't deny it. Foley had manipulated him, right along with the rest of the colony. The only difference between them and Calum was that Calum had been given a way out with the badgers, and he'd grabbed it with both hands.

"That's classic abusive behavior," Duane commented.

"The arranged marriage thing was brought up after Rip broke up with me. I told him I was a carrier because I felt it was something he should know, and he freaked out. I don't know why, and honestly, I don't care anymore. Foley used that to his advantage, though. I know that if I go back, I'll be married in a few weeks, if not sooner. I have no doubt he already has someone picked out for me, maybe a bat shifter he owes something to, maybe his beta." Or his son.

Calum remembered his son as a bully, much like his father, but the beta wasn't great, either. He wasn't sure which would be worse, but it didn't matter. He was never going back, and he wasn't marrying someone he hated.

"I realize that this is unlike the stories of the other carriers. I was lucky because no one ever hurt me," he continued. "I wasn't beaten or raped. I also didn't behave the best when I arrived here, and I apologize for that."

Thomas frowned. "You don't have to apologize for anything. Besides, you might not have been beaten, but you *were* abused. It sounds like the entire colony is being abused. You're the lucky guy who managed to escape, and knowing what you went through, I'm convinced that Foley needs to stay away from you more than ever."

"I can't say I disagree. I don't want to have to deal with him, but I hate that this forces me into hiding again. I thought that part of my life was over." But he should have known better.

Duane wanted to go all the way to the colony and find Foley to tell him what he thought of him. Hell, he was even tempted to shake the guy a few times just to make sure he understood that what he was doing wasn't right. He was controlling his colony and trying to bring Calum back into the fold, and while thankfully Calum was strong enough to resist, the other bat shifters were still in the middle of it. They deserved their freedom, but Duane didn't know enough about shifter politics to know if there was a way to make that happen.

So he stayed where he was. He suspected Calum wouldn't be happy about him storming bat territory, anyway. Duane had been horrified when Calum had pointed out that he'd had it easy. He'd been abused, and while that abuse hadn't left bruises or scars, that didn't mean it was easier to take. The situations were completely different, and Calum needed to stop comparing himself to the other carriers.

Duane rubbed his face. "So you'll keep Foley away now?" he asked Thomas.

"I already emailed him that he wasn't welcome in badger territory anymore after what he did to Calum the last time he was here. I don't think he'll need me to write again. He probably knows I talked to Calum and that Calum told me everything."

"What about Calum leaving badger territory?" Because Calum was right. He didn't deserve to be stuck in a house or even in badger territory. He should be able to live his life, and that wouldn't be possible until Foley was taken care of. But how were they going to do that?

"I'll admit that I don't like the thought of him wandering on his own, even if he stays close and only goes to the grocery store."

"*He's* right here, you know?" Calum snapped. "And he has an opinion. I won't let Foley win. I know how dangerous he is and what will happen if he gets his hands on me, but I'm here because I want to be free. Staying in the house even when I have to go to the grocery store or do something else isn't being free."

Thomas slowly nodded. "I can't say I disagree."

"Besides, it's not like I have that much time to go places. One baby is here, but Julian will give birth any day, and when he does, I'll be even busier."

"But you, Julian, and Kaspar need to eat, which means you can either go to the grocery store or have someone go for you."

"I want to be able to go."

"Then maybe you should take Duane with you."

Duane stared at Thomas in shock. He wanted to help, but considering why he was here in the forest, he hadn't expected Thomas to name him Calum's bodyguard.

"What?" Calum asked.

"Think about it. You've already told two people in your old colony that Duane's your boyfriend. That means no one would think it strange if you were to go grocery shopping with him. I realize it's not as much freedom as you want, but I'd feel better if Duane stuck by your side when you leave badger territory. Hell, I'd feel better if he stuck by your side even when you leave the house. I hate to put you in this position, and I wish I didn't have to, but I don't think Foley will let go. If he's a controlling asshole like you've told us, he has to be seething that he can't control you anymore. That means he'll try to fix that, and the only way to make that happen is to get you back. Once he has you with the colony and married, possibly even pregnant, he'll be satisfied, but not one second earlier."

Duane tightened his hands on the armrests. He didn't want to think about what would happen to Calum if Foley were to take him back, but he couldn't avoid it when Thomas said it out loud.

No one should be forced to marry anyone. No one should be forced to carry a child in any situation or circumstance. Calum deserved freedom, but it looked like they'd need to take care of Foley and the colony before he could have it.

How were they supposed to do that?

"I don't need a babysitter," Calum said.

"I agree, but that's not why Duane will be with you. He'll be your bodyguard, not your babysitter."

"They're the same thing."

"Not unless your babysitter spent years in the human military."

The two of them looked at Duane, and he realized they were waiting for an answer. "I'll do whatever it takes to keep Calum safe," he promised. "And you're not wrong. Foley already thinks we're together. He won't be surprised to see me with Calum out of badger territory, especially at the grocery store."

Calum was frowning. "But I'm not the reason you're here.

You have a job to do, and it's not following me around."

"My job is to protect shifters. It's why I was hired and why I'm being paid. Sure, I was supposed to protect you guys from humans, but it doesn't mean I can't help protect you from a shifter."

"And while you wouldn't stand a chance against some of the other alphas, like Morris, Foley's shifted form is small. He won't try attacking you as a bat, and if he does so as a human, I have no doubt you'll have the upper hand," Thomas said.

"This is going to be a disaster," Calum muttered.

Duane couldn't say he disagreed. Even if he won whatever fight Foley was raring for, he was in shifter territory. He was here to protect them, not to fight with them, but how could he stay out of this? Calum needed his help, and Duane wanted to be there for him and to make sure nothing happened to Calum and that he wasn't forced into anything he didn't want—although he supposed that pushing him on Calum *was* forcing him to accept a bodyguard.

But until he was safe, Duane would stick with him. He didn't need Thomas's order to do so.

"Fine," Calum said with a huff. "He can be my bodyguard. I don't like this, though."

Thomas grinned. "We're very much aware of that."

"And I'll be vocal about it."

"I didn't expect anything else from you." Thomas's smile vanished. "I just want to keep you safe, Calum. If that means keeping you in badger territory for a while, I'll do it. If it means asking someone to stay with you at all times and pro-tect you, I'll do that. I have faith in Duane, and I'll feel better knowing that even if Foley finds you again, you won't face him on your own."

Calum still didn't look happy, but at least he'd softened. Duane felt that was all they could have asked for.

Calum got to his feet suddenly, startling Duane. He needed

to keep a better eye on the bat shifter if he was going to keep him safe.

"I'm going home," Calum declared. "Julian and Kaspar need me, and I have things to do."

He didn't even look at Duane as he strode out of the room. Duane and Thomas exchanged a glance, and Thomas tilted his chin toward the door.

"You should probably follow him and try talking to him. He's clearly unhappy, but this is necessary."

Duane agreed, which was one of the reasons he got to his feet and followed Calum. Maybe if they talked, Calum would understand that Duane only wanted the best for him.

Even though he didn't understand why he felt that way.

Calum was glad to be outside and away from Thomas and Duane. They hadn't reacted the way he'd thought they would, and he had no idea how to deal with that. He'd believed they'd agree with him that what he'd gone through wasn't that bad. Instead, Thomas had declared that Calum had been abused, but Calum couldn't see it.

Yes, Foley was a controlling asshole, but as far as Calum knew, he'd never hurt anyone. Was what he was doing really abuse? It didn't feel like it, next to what some of the other carriers had gone through. Calum had been blaming himself for behaving like an asshole and making his situation worse, but now he had doubts. He didn't know what to think.

The one thing he knew how he felt about was the fact that he was stuck. Even though he was allowed to leave badger territory, he could only do so with Duane by his side. He'd come so far, yet, he still needed someone to hover over him.

He wasn't sure how to feel about the fact that that person would be Duane. He liked Duane and wanted to spend more time with him, but he was confused. Why did he feel that way? Was it just because Duane was hot? They didn't know each other, so there was no way for Calum to know if Duane was a good person. Not many people would have stepped in at the grocery store, though, and even fewer of them would have done so when Foley had been there. Duane had been present for Calum every time he needed his support to deal with the colony.

"Calum!"

Duane's voice made Calum stop. He wasn't sure he wanted to talk to the human, but he could imagine both of them running through the forest with Duane begging him to stop. Calum wasn't one to draw attention, and he didn't want to start today. Besides, he had a few questions for Duane. He might as well ask them now.

Duane ran toward Calum. He wasn't even out of breath when he reached him, and Calum narrowed his eyes at him. He supposed that made sense, since Duane was highly trained, but he didn't like it.

"Yes?" he asked.

"I don't want to bother you. I just thought you might have questions."

"Why are you doing this?" That was the main thing Calum wanted an answer to.

Thankfully, Duane didn't hesitate. "I told you. I'm here to protect shifters, and you're a shifter."

But Calum wasn't satisfied. "To protect me, yes, but not to be my boyfriend."

Duane grinned. "Fake boyfriend."

Calum briefly wondered if they could become real boy-friends, but he had too many things to worry over right now to add a possible relationship. Besides, what would happen once Duane spent a little time around here? Calum had no idea what the human world was really like, but he'd seen it on TV, and he could imagine how much better it was than the forest. There was no way any human would stick around for long, including Duane. If they got together, what would Calum do once Duane decided to leave?

Calum's heart had broken when Rip had dumped him. He didn't want to feel that way ever again, even though he doubted Duane would be as nasty about it as Rip had been.

"You being a guard makes sense. You being my fake boyfriend doesn't. Why would you want to be stuck with this kind of job?"

Thankfully, Duane didn't brush off Calum right away. He took a few moments to think over his answer, and it made Calum feel better.

"I've always been a protector," Duane eventually said. "It's one of the reasons I went into the military. I wanted to protect my country, and even more, my father and my brother. When I left, I knew I wanted to do something similar, but without all the rules and blood."

Calum snorted. "You'll see plenty of blood if Foley continues acting like an idiot."

"I'll deal with it. I always felt shifters should be free, and while there's nothing I can do to help with that situation, I can be here for you. You need help, and I can provide it."

"I don't like feeling useless and weak."

"No one said you were useless and weak."

They'd reached the house, but Calum still didn't like any of this. "Well, you and Thomas have made me feel that way." He was aware his voice was rising, but he was *so* angry. It wasn't even at Duane, although the poor man was taking the brunt of it. No, Calum was angry at Foley, who was still controlling his life even though Calum had left.

Duane raised his hands. "I understand, and I wish I could step away from this, but do you really want to risk it?"

"Maybe I should learn how to defend myself, then. I don't need anyone to do it for me."

"You might not need it, but that doesn't mean you shouldn't have help. Would you feel this way if someone else was in your place? Maybe one of your friends? I promise I'll do my best to stay out of your way, but it would be easier for me to be by your side. Let me be your fake boyfriend, Calum."

"Why do you need a fake boyfriend?" a voice asked.

Calum turned to find Julian sitting on the porch. He had a hand on his stomach and looked tired, but his eyes glittered. He was also smiling, which told Calum he'd heard the conversation and wouldn't hesitate to use it against him.

"I don't," Calum snapped.

Julian and Kaspar had stopped being offended by Calum's tone long ago. They knew how much he loved them, no matter how abrasive he was.

Julian started getting to his feet, but he was struggling. Before Calum could step in, Duane climbed the porch steps two by two and went to stand next to Julian. He helped him to his feet, and when Julian looked up at him, Calum could have sworn his cheeks were flushed.

"Thank you," Julian said. "I don't think I've ever met you before. I'm Julian."

"Duane."

"Well, Duane, why are you Calum's fake boyfriend?"

"Because his ex-alpha is trying to get him back, and both Thomas and I agree he's dangerous. We don't want to risk it, so when Calum needs to leave badger territory, I'll go with him. He already told his ex-alpha I'm his boyfriend, so it works out perfectly."

Calum glared at Duane. Did he *have* to blurt everything out like that? Now Julian would be worried, and that was the last thing he needed days before giving birth.

Julian's eyes sparkled. "And where are you living right now?"

"With the other human guards, although Thomas told me

that he wants me to choose an empty house and make it mine."

Calum knew Julian was planning something, but it was too late because Julian asked, "Why don't you move in with us for the moment? If you're Calum's boyfriend, it would make sense for you to live with us."

"It's not necessary," Calum said. "He only needs to be with me when I'm out of badger territory."

"Actually, Thomas said he wanted me with you even inside badger territory. Living here would be perfect," Duane said.

Calum groaned. Fuck his life.

Chapter Eight

Moving in with Julian and Kaspar had been a big change for Calum, and he hated changes. Having Duane around the house changed everything once again, although Calum supposed he couldn't complain. With one of the babies already born, things had changed. It wasn't just Duane, no matter how much Calum wished he could blame him for all of it.

Since he had no intention of having a conversation with Duane, he'd taken to avoiding him. That had been easy when Duane lived with the other guards, but it was almost impossible now that he was in the same house. Calum hated it, but he'd started getting up early to get breakfast ready before Duane could get back from his run, and as soon as he heard Duane's footsteps, he vanished back into his bedroom. It was annoying, and it meant he wasn't helping Julian and Kaspar as much, but he didn't know how else to deal with this.

He didn't know what to do about the fact that he wanted Duane to be his actual boyfriend, not just a fake one.

Calum was glad when Cal started crying. He rushed out of his bedroom, hoping he'd get to Cal before he woke his fathers, who were having a nap. His crying cut off, though, which meant Calum was too late. He still stepped into the nursery to see if Kaspar needed anything, but to his surprise, Kaspar wasn't the one holding his son.

Duane was.

Cal looked tiny in Duane's broad hands. Duane could hurt him, but even though Calum didn't know him, he was sure

Duane would never do something like that. The way he was cradling Cal against his chest was proof.

Duane started to turn, and Calum quickly stepped back into the hallway. He had no idea what was happening, but he was curious.

"What's the problem, little guy?" Duane asked, his voice rumbling.

Calum found himself relaxing at the sound. He couldn't imagine Cal not feeling the same.

"You don't smell like you need a diaper change, but maybe I should check. Or should I take you to your dad? But he's sleeping, and considering how many times you wake up during the night, he needs at least another hour. You think you can be good with me during that time?"

Calum closed his eyes. This shouldn't be as adorable as it was, dammit. Duane wasn't here to be Cal's babysitter. He wasn't here to cradle Cal in his arms and talk to him as softly as he was.

Why the fuck was Calum jealous of the baby?

"Oh," another voice said, and Calum realized Julian had come in through the connecting door between his bedroom and the nursery.

"Sorry about this," Duane said. "I was in the hallway when he started crying. I was hoping you and Kaspar would get some more sleep."

"Well, you don't have to worry. I'm awake, and you can give Cal to me."

"I'll go warm some milk, if that's okay with you."

"It would be perfect."

Calum's eyes widened when he realized Duane would have to walk past him. He looked around, saw that the closet door was slightly open, and threw himself into it. He didn't have the time to close it fully before Duane walked into the hallway, but he huddled back, and it was enough that Duane didn't see him.

Calum's heart raced. Why was he hiding like an idiot? Who cared if he was in the hallway listening to Duane?

"You can come out," Julian said from the open door of the nursery.

Calum huffed. "How did you know?" he asked as he left the closet and firmly closed the door behind himself.

"I heard you. Why are you avoiding Duane?"

Calum sighed. Julian was one of his best friends, and at the same time, he was kind of a father figure to him. Calum was closer to him than he'd ever been to his own father, and he could see Julian was worried about him. "I don't know what to do with him."

Julian's eyes sparkled. "Well, I could give you a few ideas."

"Please, don't." It would be like getting sex advice from his father. "It's just that he's human, and eventually he'll return home. I don't think my heart can deal with that again."

Julian's expression turned more serious. "I understand. You don't have to throw yourself into anything you're not ready for. But you're young, Calum. You might meet the man of your dreams now, but you might also not meet him for years. Duane might be that guy, but he also might not be. Not all relationships are made to last. Maybe you should give Duane a chance. Whether or not he decides to go home, he can be something for you right now."

"He's already my bodyguard," Calum pointed out.

"But you want him to be so much more, don't you?"

"I don't know. I just know that I want him and that I have no idea how to deal with that."

A sound made Calum turn toward the stairs. Duane stood there with wide eyes, staring at Calum while holding Cal's bottle. Calum sucked in a breath. Duane had heard him, hadn't he? He knew how Calum felt about him, and Calum would have to deal with him knowing.

But not right now.

Calum turned and rushed toward his bedroom. He heard Duane call out for him, but he didn't stop or slow down. He didn't want to find out that Duane didn't see him that way. He wanted to be safe in his bedroom, and when he slammed the door shut behind himself, he could finally breathe.

But how long would that last?

Duane stood there like an idiot, even after he'd heard Calum say he wanted him. Why had Calum run away? What the fuck was happening?

"Duane?" Julian asked softly.

That got Duane to move again. He offered Julian the bottle, and Julian took it with a smile.

"Why don't you come with me into the nursery?" Julian asked.

He walked back into the room without checking if Duane was following him. Duane went because he had no idea what else to do.

He had no idea what to do with Calum, either.

Julian sat in the chair by the window and offered the bottle to the baby, who latched on fiercely. Duane leaned against the wall, unsure what he should do. It was clear Julian wanted to talk to him, and it was probably about Calum.

"You heard what he said," Julian said. His tone wasn't accusing, which was good.

"I didn't mean to. I was coming back up and heard you talking to him, but I didn't realize the conversation was so private. I'd have gone back downstairs if I had."

"Maybe it's good that you didn't."

"How can it be good? Calum ran away and locked himself in his bedroom." Duane hadn't been making progress with Calum, but they also hadn't been going backward. He was pretty sure they had just now, though.

"It's what he does," Julian said with a smile. "I don't know what happened to him with the colony. You might know more than I do by now. What I do know is that since he arrived in badger territory, he's been pushing people away. For a long time, that included Kaspar and me. Things have changed, but then we've been living together for a while. When I heard that you were supposed to be his fake boyfriend, I hoped it meant he'd be more open with you."

"I can't see that happening."

"Maybe not, but maybe yes. You already have an effect on him I haven't seen anyone else have."

"He's been avoiding me."

"Which means he feels something. The fact that he confessed he wants you isn't a surprise. Maybe it's time for the two of you to be aware of it and for you to confront him over it."

"But I *didn't* confront him over it."

"Not yet. I have no doubt he'll continue avoiding you. If you want to talk to him, you'll have to push hard. He needs to stop hiding, though."

"It can't be easy when he knows his old alpha is after him." Duane wasn't sure how he'd deal with it if he were in Calum's place.

"I agree, but that's not all he's hiding from. I love him like a son, and I love that he lives with Kaspar and me and helps us with the baby. I'm overwhelmed as it is, and I can only imagine what it'll be like when we have two babies. But I'm not blind, and I can see that he's using our situation to hide from the rest of the cete. Even though his presence is necessary, he's doing too much. It's not just that he wants us to see that he can help so we won't kick him out, but also that it's a way for him to stay away from everyone else. That's not good for him. He's only twenty-one and has his entire life in front of him. As difficult as it is at the moment, he should enjoy it, not hide from it."

Duane rubbed the back of his neck. "I can't say I disagree with you, but I'm not sure what my role is in all of this beyond protecting him."

"What do you want from him?"

"To spend time with him. To get to know him."

"And you're planning to stay with the cete, right?"

"If I can, yes. There's not much for me in the human world apart from my brother and father, and they're used to being without me. I thought I could find a place here."

"And I think you did. The question is if you want Calum to be part of your life here."

Duane knew the answer to that. "I do."

"Then you have to show him, and please, tell him you're not going anywhere. One of the main reasons he's staying away from you is that he's terrified you'll leave him behind. He doesn't want his heart to break, and I understand. He's already been through so much pain that it's easier to hide so he doesn't have to go through it again."

Everything Julian was saying sounded good, but Duane had doubts. "How am I supposed to tell him all of this when he won't talk to me? I doubt that the fact that I heard your conversation will change how he's been avoiding me."

"It won't. You need to show him that you're here to stay and that you care about him."

"How do I do that?"

"Do something for him. He's not used to having someone care for him. He's the one doing all the caring when it comes to Kaspar and me, and I suspect that even when he was with the colony, most people dismissed him. He does a lot for everyone to show us he's useful and to convince us to keep him with us, and maybe it's time someone does something for him."

"Like what?"

Julian grinned. "You're going to have to figure that out. I think I've already helped you enough, and I can't do all the work for you."

He wasn't wrong. The problem was that Duane had no idea where to start, especially when it came to Calum, who was so prickly and eager to push him away.

But he'd find a way to Calum's heart. He'd already liked Calum before, and watching him around the house, with Julian and Kaspar, and hearing Julian talk about him, added tiny details to the image Duane had of him. He couldn't wait to find out more, and for that to happen, he'd have to break through Calum's shell. It would be a challenge, but Duane wasn't afraid of those.

Especially when the reward would be Calum.

Unfortunately, Calum couldn't hide in his bedroom for the rest of the day, so in the late afternoon, he stepped out. He needed to cook dinner, and it was getting late. It wouldn't do anyone any good if he skirted his responsibilities, least of all Kaspar and Julian. They both needed their strength, and making sure they got everything they needed was why Calum was here.

But as soon as he stepped out of his bedroom, he could smell something cooking. He frowned, wondering if Duane had taken over the job. That wasn't why he was here, but there wasn't much to do to keep Calum safe. Calum hadn't left the house again, so the only thing attacking him were dust bunnies.

Knowing someone else was cooking made Calum hesitate. If it was Duane, he wasn't sure he wanted to see him. He'd have to eventually, though. He supposed he might as well get it over with now.

He sucked in a breath and made his way downstairs. The house was silent, but it wasn't odd for this time of day. The baby woke up every two hours or so, so Kaspar napped every chance he got. As for Julian, he was spending a lot of his time in bed resting, too. Calum had no idea what Duane usually did when he was home, but he might be about to find out.

He stepped into the kitchen, ready to apologize. That was the only thing he could think of when it came to what Duane had heard. It couldn't be a surprise to Duane that some people found him attractive. One of those people was Calum, but it didn't mean they had to do anything. Calum wasn't an idiot, and he understood there was no way Duane would want someone like him. Even if Duane decided to stay in the forest for the long term, he could have someone stronger who didn't struggle with his past, present, and future.

But it wasn't Duane in the kitchen. Julian stood in front of the stove, his bump covered by an apron. For a few seconds, Calum stared. Then he rushed forward.

"What are you doing?" he asked. "This is my job, not yours."

Julian rolled his eyes. "I know how to cook. I had to do so for years in the forest, and I didn't have a stove then."

"But it's my job."

"But you need to rest sometimes."

"I'm not the one heavily pregnant. I don't need rest."

"Everyone needs rest." Julian's expression softened. "You worry about us too much. Sometimes, it's overwhelming. I don't blame you for that, but I wish you'd realize that I'm an adult and can take care of myself."

Calum stepped back. He knew he could be overwhelming, but he didn't know what else to do. He was here to help Kaspar and Julian. What good was he to them if he didn't do that?

Julian frowned. "I can already see what you're thinking, and you need to stop."

Calum shook his head. "I don't know what you're talking about."

"You know what I'm talking about. Cleaning and cooking aren't the reason you're here. You're here because we're a family, and I need you to understand it and accept it. Besides, Duane already did most of the work. I'll be fine finishing up and taking a plate up to Kaspar. Hell, maybe he'll even come downstairs. Do you know how long it's been since we had a nice dinner together?"

Calum did, because he'd been here for most of their dinners over the past few months. "What do you mean, Duane did most of the work?"

"He started dinner. He's in his bedroom getting ready, but he should be downstairs soon." Julian looked Calum up and down. "You should probably get changed."

"What are you talking about?"

"I'd like to take you out for dinner," Duane said from behind Calum.

Calum tensed. He hadn't heard Duane, but that wasn't a surprise since he was focused on the conversation with Julian. He didn't understand what Duane was saying, though.

He slowly turned to look at him and almost swallowed his tongue. Duane always wore jeans and a t-shirt or the new uniform the human guards wore. Looking at him right now shouldn't have been anything new since once again, he wore jeans, but Calum couldn't look away from the button-up shirt that stretched over Duane's chest.

How could anyone be so handsome?

"Calum?" Julian gently prodded.

Calum shook himself. "Why do you want to take me out to dinner?" he asked Duane. After hearing his conversation with Julian, he thought Duane might start avoiding him.

"Well, for one, Julian, Kaspar, and I agreed that you could do with a night away from the house to do whatever you want. You've been taking good care of them and the baby, but they can't be your entire life."

"They can be whatever I say they are," Calum snapped. He was *so* over people telling him what to do. If he decided he never wanted to leave this house, that was what he'd do, and no one would be able to force him otherwise.

Duane raised his hands. He behaved almost as if Calum was a dangerous wild animal, which probably made sense, considering how he was behaving. He felt slightly guilty, but he didn't need anyone's pity. He also didn't need anyone to distract him from his job, which was taking care of Kaspar and Julian.

"You can decide whatever you want, and if you want to stay home, it's perfectly fine. I just thought it would be nice to have someone else cook for you tonight, maybe for you to choose something you normally don't eat. I understand you're nervous about going into town, and I don't blame you, but I'll be with you."

Calum thought about it. "Are you taking me out so everyone will think we're a couple?" It would make sense, and he should have realized that sooner.

Of course Duane and Thomas wanted people to see them together. It would make their story look even more true, which meant Foley might stay away.

"That wasn't my intention," Duane said. "I'd like to take you to dinner because I thought it would be something nice to do for you."

"And why would you want to do something nice for me? You don't know me."

"But I do," Julian said. He stepped closer and gently touched Calum's forearm. "You always think of everyone first and never of yourself. When Kaspar and I try to do something for you, you won't let us."

Calum looked at the floor and shuffled his feet. "I'm sorry

if I'm overbearing."

Julian chuckled. "You can be a bit, sometimes, but that's not what I'm talking about. Kaspar and I are happy to have you with us and relieved you're helping us. We can't be your entire life, though. Eventually, I'll give birth, and somewhere down the line, the babies will grow up, and they won't need us as much as they do now. I don't want your entire life to revolve around us. We're your family, and that won't ever change, but you need more."

Calum was still skeptical. "And that more is Duane?"

Julian's eyes glittered. "I'm sure that if you want that to happen, he'll be happy to help. We just want you to take some time to yourself, though. If you go out with Duane, you won't have to think of me, dinner, or the baby for a while. Kaspar and I will be fine. Cal is our son, after all, and I know how to take care of a baby. I'm sure we can do without you for a few hours, and I want you to have fun."

Calum wasn't sure he knew what having fun was like. He couldn't remember the last time he'd had fun, although watching movies with Kaspar and Julian had always been nice. Talking to them was, too, but he didn't know what to expect of dinner with Duane.

He looked at the man again. Duane had clearly put some thought into the way he'd dressed tonight, and Calum wondered why. Did he want to impress him? It didn't make sense, but a lot of things didn't make sense in Calum's life right now.

Duane wasn't just wearing a dress shirt that molded his muscles and made Calum want to touch him. He'd shaved, and his hair was neatly combed. Unless Calum was mistaken, he'd put on some cologne, but thankfully, it wasn't offensive to Calum's shifter nose. It was almost as if Duane was trying to impress Calum, and Calum didn't understand why.

But maybe he didn't have to.

Watching Calum be so hesitant over something as simple as having dinner out was painful. Maybe it was more because of Duane than dinner itself, but Duane wasn't sure what he could do to fix that. He supposed Calum could go out by himself, but would he want to?

Besides, this dinner was important to Duane. After talking with Julian, he could see Julian was right. Calum did a lot for other people and very little for himself. It was almost as if he was afraid that someone would berate him for it and kick him out if he did. Duane didn't know Julian and Kaspar well yet, but even he could tell they'd never do something like that.

"Go out and have fun," Julian pushed again. "We'll still be here by the time you're back. It would only be a few hours, and I promise to call if anything happens."

Calum turned to him again. "Even if you go into labor? Because Kaspar didn't tell us right away."

"That's because he didn't recognize it, but I've been through this once already, remember? I promise you'll be the second person I tell if I go into labor."

Calum wrinkled his nose. "Third. Tell Kaspar, call Cynthia, then call me. She'll be more useful than me."

"I'll do that, then."

It sounded like they were doing this. Duane told himself it was just dinner between friends, but he couldn't deny he hoped something more would happen. Maybe not today, but eventually, he wanted Calum to see him as something more than a fake boyfriend.

Maybe a real boyfriend.

Duane had been intrigued by Calum since the first time he met him at the grocery store. That feeling had grown since he'd met Calum again and had started living with him and the others, and he was eager to find out more about the guy he had a crush on. Calum had a hard exterior and was prickly and snarky, but it was easy to see that deep inside, he was soft and wanted to be loved. It wasn't only in a partner kind of way, either. From what Duane had seen, Calum yearned for family, and Kaspar and Julian were more than happy to provide him with that. Duane would be, too, once Calum was ready.

But first, dinner.

"Do you want to change before we go out?" he asked.

Calum looked down at his jeans and sweater. "Do I need to?"

"Not if you don't want to. I thought we could grab dinner, ice cream, and maybe a movie."

"We'll be away more than a few hours if we do that."

Julian huffed. "Go with the man, Calum. I promised I'd call you if anything happened, and I meant it. Stop worrying about Kaspar and me for a moment. You're not our father." He winked. "That would be just too weird."

Calum shuddered dramatically, but he was smiling. Duane didn't fully understand the relationship between Calum, Julian, and Kaspar, but it was clear they loved each other and that it was important to Calum.

"I'll go wash up quick," Calum said. "Wait here."

"I will," Duane promised.

Thankfully, he didn't have to wait long, because Julian kept peering at him as if he wanted to ask what his intentions were. He stopped himself every time, but it was clear that he viewed Calum as a son. Besides, he'd told Duane that much a few hours ago. Julian wanted Calum to be happy, and he seemed to think Duane would be able to help with that. Duane wasn't sure about that, but he was ready to try. Hopefully, dinner and a movie would only be the first step.

When Calum came back, he was wearing different clothes, but still jeans and a sweater. His hair was damp, and his cheeks were flushed. The way he looked made Duane want to grab him and drag him to his bedroom instead of going out, but he'd made a promise, and he'd keep it.

Hopefully, they'd have time to be together that way in the future. Duane hoped this wasn't the only time they went out.

He and Julian had planned everything out, so Duane knew exactly where to go. "Julian told me you enjoy Italian food," he said as he drove them toward Northwood. The city was a bit far, but it would give them time to talk.

"Who doesn't like Italian food?" Calum asked.

"True. I missed that a lot when I was overseas."

"You were in the military."

"I was."

"How was it? You got to leave your home and travel."

And Calum never had, because shifters were stuck here. "Well, I wasn't traveling for pleasure. It was a job, and it wasn't great."

"Why did you do it, then?"

"Because I wanted to protect my family. I did that by protecting my country."

Calum nodded. "It's good that you have a family." He sounded wistful.

"You have a family, too. Julian was very insistent on that point."

"I know they love me, but I can't help but wonder if I'll still have a place with them once the second baby is born. Maybe Kaspar and Julian will want to be a real family and ask me to leave."

Calum snapped his mouth shut as if he regretted saying that out loud, but he shouldn't. Duane liked knowing what Calum was thinking. "I don't think there's any chance of that happening. You do a lot for them, but that's not why they love you. You're part of their life, and that's not going to change."

"I hope so."

Calum had already lost so much. He deserved everything

he wanted, be that a family, a boyfriend, a job, or anything else. There wasn't much Duane could do to give it to him, except for maybe the boyfriend part. Even if they never became anything more than friends, Duane wanted to be there for Calum, to protect him, and to make him happy. He wasn't sure he could do it, but he was certainly going to try.

"So you're taking me to eat Italian?" Calum asked.

"I am, and the restaurant has ice cream, too, so we can get that for dessert."

"Then a movie?"

"If you want, but I'd rather you choose what you want to do. The movie was just an idea." Since Calum was nervous about leaving Julian and Kaspar alone for too long, maybe a movie at the theater wasn't the best idea. That wasn't the only way to watch movies, though. "Or we could go home and watch a movie there."

Calum frowned. "It wouldn't be the same."

"Probably not, but we could make it nice, make some popcorn, turn off the lights, things like that. I know you're nervous about leaving Julian alone so close to his due date, and I want you to be comfortable."

Duane could feel Calum watching him, but he kept his focus on the road. In most circumstances, Calum wasn't shy about telling people what he thought. The only part of himself he kept hidden was a deep fear of being abandoned by the people he now considered friends and family. That was why he did everything he could to make himself useful. He didn't hold back anything else, though, so Duane wasn't surprised when he started speaking again.

"I don't understand why you're doing this, but thank you," he murmured.

Duane grinned. "There's nothing to thank me for."

"No one's ever taken me out for dinner. It's almost like a date."

Duane licked his lips. Now felt like the perfect time to take a risk, and he hoped it would pay off. "It could be a date if you wanted it to be."

There was a moment of silence, and Duane told himself Calum wasn't going to say no.

"You'd want to go on a date with me?" Calum asked.

"Yes, and not because I'm your fake boyfriend. I like you." It was better to say those things out loud. Calum needed to hear them.

Sure enough, when Duane peeked at him, the smile spreading Calum's lips was the most beautiful thing Duane had ever seen. It had only taken him a few words to make Calum happy.

And Duane wanted to do so for the rest of his life.

Chapter Nine

Julian was lucky Calum loved him. If he didn't, he wouldn't be outside in the cold, hanging up the laundry. Julian liked it when it was line dried, probably because he hadn't had a choice about it for most of his life. He said something about the dryer irritating his skin, and while Calum wasn't sure if that was true, he could be cold for a few moments to hang up Julian's clothing.

Besides, being outside on his own gave him the opportunity to think about Duane. The date they'd been on a few days ago had been nice, but it had left Calum even more confused about what they were doing.

Surely Duane wouldn't have said he wanted it to be a date if he didn't like Calum. Calum had a hard time wrapping his mind around the fact that someone could like him that way, though. He'd been pushing everyone away, from Thomas to Julian and Kaspar, to Duane. He didn't understand how anyone could like him, especially not a human who knew what had happened to him.

No one had loved Calum enough to care about him and what he wanted. He wasn't angry at his parents, who wouldn't have been able to do much against their alpha, but Foley was supposed to protect him, not force him to marry someone he didn't want. He was supposed to make sure Calum was happy and had what he needed, but instead, he was like all those other alphas who'd been taken down. The only difference was that Foley hadn't been obvious about how bad he was, which was probably the only reason he was still at the head of the colony.

The bats wouldn't do anything to change that. Foley had them under his thumb, which made sense since he was the alpha. As for the council, they didn't usually intervene in this kind of situation. They'd stepped in to help the carriers, but they wouldn't choose a new alpha for the bats. No, if the alpha was going to change, the bats would have to do that themselves, and it wasn't something Calum could see them doing.

It wasn't his problem anymore. He wasn't a colony member, and he never would be again. That was one thing he was sure of when it came to his future. If somehow Foley managed to get to him, Calum would rather kill himself than go along with whatever he was planning.

But Calum had to believe he was safe in badger territory. Foley might be an asshole, but he wasn't stupid. Coming into badger territory again, especially after Thomas had told him to stay away, would be idiotic. It might start a war between the badgers and the bats, and Calum had no doubt the badgers would win if things came to that. They had allies, many more than the bats could ever dream of.

Calum should focus on his new life. He was lucky to have an opportunity like the one Thomas had given him, and he needed to stop pushing people away. So what if they hurt him? He'd survived until now, and he could continue doing so. He didn't think everyone would abandon him, but he'd find a way to make it even if they did. He could move to Northwood, find a job, and build a new life.

But he hoped he wouldn't have to. Even though he was surrounded by people, he was lonely, and it was entirely his fault for pushing everyone away. It was hard to convince himself that the people around him weren't going to abandon him, but it had been months, and maybe, he could finally admit the truth.

He wasn't alone in the world.

He had Thomas, who'd welcomed him when others would have kicked him out. He had Julian and Kaspar, who were grateful for his help but also for his presence in their life because they loved him. He had Kari, Calder, and the other carriers. Hell, he was starting to think he even had Duane, although he wasn't sure where that was going.

But he wasn't alone, and that was what he needed to focus on.

The sound of someone walking in the snow made him turn. He was ready to admonish Kaspar or Julian if it was them because they needed to stay in the warm house, but the footsteps came from the forest, not from the house. It could be Kari visiting his father or any other member of the cete, but it wasn't.

It was Foley, and he wasn't alone.

Calum tried to remember the name of the man with him. The colony was numerous, and while Calum had tried his best to stay away from the alpha and his people, especially after Foley had found out he was a carrier, everyone knew who the alpha was and that his authority was absolute. The guy with him didn't look like someone Calum knew, though.

So what was he? More importantly, how had Foley managed to sneak into badger territory?

"Good morning," Foley said as if he wasn't doing something he'd been told not to do.

He hadn't just snuck into badger territory. He was also talking to Calum, even after Calum had told him he didn't want to see him again.

"You need to leave," Calum told him.

"Not even a hello? I'm your alpha, Calum. You should be more respectful."

Calum was angry, and Foley's words stoked that anger. "You're *not* my alpha. You haven't been in months, and that's not going to change. *Thomas* is my alpha now, and he's a hundred times the man you'll ever be."

Foley opened his arms. "Yet he's not here to protect you. He doesn't even know we walked into his territory without anyone stopping us."

It wasn't like the various territories were separated by fences or anything like that. The forest was wide open, but shifters knew they had entered someone else's territory from the scent. Besides, Foley knew what he was doing. He'd come for Calum, and Calum wondered why he was so obsessed with him.

"You need to leave," he snapped when Foley stepped even closer.

"And who's going to force me? You? Look around, Calum. You're all alone, and there are two of us. Besides, you're a carrier." Foley straightened his back. "You'll obey my orders, and you'll do it with a smile on your face." He looked at the guy standing next to him. "Patrick is here for you."

"Who the fuck is Patrick?"

Foley tsked. "I didn't teach you that language."

"You didn't teach me anything, asshole."

"Well, no matter. I'm sure Patrick will teach you manners once the two of you are married."

Calum sucked in a breath of cold air. So this was the guy he'd been supposed to marry. He didn't think Foley had ever told him his name.

Patrick wasn't ugly, but his expression was. He was in his mid to late forties, and there was no way for Calum to know what kind of shifter he was. His hair was almost entirely gray, and his dark eyes were hard as they looked at Calum. The way he was staring made Calum feel like a piece of meat at the grocery store.

"You didn't say he'd be so mouthy," Patrick said.

"Does it matter? You can do whatever you want with him. You'll find a way to teach him not to open his mouth when he's not told to speak." Foley looked around. "We should grab him. Someone is bound to come eventually."

"How did you find me? How did you know I live here?" Calum was desperately trying to use up some time.

He didn't want Kaspar or Julian to intervene, and he wasn't sure where Duane was. He hadn't told him he was going to work, so it was possible he was at the house, but would he notice something was happening? Besides, while Foley was a bat shifter and unable to hurt Duane in his shifted form, there was no way to know about Patrick. Calum would never forgive himself if something happened to Duane because of him.

Foley waved his hand at the forest. "Your scent is all over the place. Now, be a good boy and come with us. If you do, we won't hurt your friends."

Calum didn't believe him. The worst thing he could do was to go along with what Foley wanted, which meant that the *best* thing he could do was the opposite.

So he shifted. It was easy for him to get out of his clothes. He abandoned them in the snow and flew toward the house, but he could hear Foley coming after him. He was running for now, but what would happen when he shifted?

Calum was distracted, which explained why he didn't see the wall in front of him. There wasn't supposed to be a wall there, and when he slammed against it, it took him a second to realize that. Then a warm hand cupped him, and he realized what had happened.

Duane was here.

Duane was pissed. He kept a hand around Calum's trembling body and glared at the asshole who'd been his alpha. Foley shouldn't be anyone's boss.

When he'd heard voices outside, he'd expected Julian or

Kaspar to be out there with Calum. He'd seen Calum earlier, so he knew Calum was out there hanging up the laundry. Apparently Julian liked when it was line dried, which seemed like a complication when it was so cold and there was snow on the ground, but who was Duane to argue?

But it wasn't Kaspar or Julian out there with Calum. It was Foley and another guy, and both of them looked angry.

There was no way they could be angrier than Duane.

"What the fuck are you doing here?" he demanded to know.

"We're here to retrieve my colony member," Foley said as if the meeting with Thomas and Alex hadn't happened.

Hadn't Thomas been clear that he didn't want Foley in his territory again? The guy was itching for a fight, and Duane was ready to give it to him. He could easily beat the guy, but he wasn't sure about the other one. Foley was a bat shifter, so he'd be similar to Calum in size. If he was smart, he wouldn't shift to fight Duane. The other guy could be a bear, a bobcat, a coyote, or any other animal that would be dangerous for Duane to fight. Unfortunately, Duane was human, so there wasn't much he'd be able to do against a bear shifter.

"Hand him over, and we'll leave," the other guy said.

Was he stupid? He had to be. "I'm not handing over anyone. Calum is his own person and able to make his own decisions. I know the laws. You can't force him into anything, be it going back to the colony or marrying someone."

"I can force him to do whatever I want," Foley snapped. "He's mine."

Duane scoffed. "Can you read? Because if you can, you should go over the new laws. Your council approved them. Carriers have as many rights as any other shifter, which means that if Calum doesn't want to go with you, no one can force him to. You don't want to go, do you, Calum?" Duane asked, looking down.

Calum's bat form was a cute little thing. His wings and ears were almost black, but his soft fur was a dark brown. Duane could see sharp teeth in his mouth, but Calum wouldn't bite him, just like he wasn't digging his claws into Duane's chest. He was just clinging to him, clearly terrified he'd be taken away.

Duane wouldn't allow anyone to hurt him, least of all Foley.

"You're human. You'll never be enough for a shifter, not even for him."

Duane grinned. "Won't I? Because I'm already enough for Calum. We're together, remember?"

Foley hissed and looked back at the other guy, who now looked pissed. "You didn't tell me he had someone," the guy said.

"He's human. He doesn't matter."

"It looks like he does."

Duane had no idea what was happening between those two, but he didn't care. He took advantage of their distraction to take out his phone and speed-dial Thomas. Thomas had already answered by the time Foley noticed what he was doing.

Duane grinned at him, making sure to show him his teeth. He might not be a shifter, but he was a fighter, and he wanted Foley to know that.

"Hey, Thomas, we have a problem here."

"What's going on?" Thomas sounded worried.

Duane agreed. He'd been with the badgers long enough that he realized it would be impossible for them to protect every inch of their borders, especially the inside borders. There would always be a way for other shifters to sneak into their territory as long as they chose a spot the badger patrols didn't reach. That was no doubt what Foley had done, but Duane didn't like the fact that he'd managed to get all the way to the house. It was one thing for him to sneak into badger territory, but it was entirely different for him to get to the house where a heavily pregnant man, a newborn child, and Calum lived.

"I'm home with Calum, and Foley somehow found his way to the house. He was trying to take Calum away."

Thomas swore. "I'll be right there."

Duane held Foley's gaze as he answered. "I doubt you'll find him here when you reach us, but we'll see you in a few moments."

"You'll regret this," Foley hissed.

Duane grinned at him. "Not as much as you will if you don't leave before Thomas gets here. I doubt he's coming alone."

Foley and his friend looked at each other. The friend was the first to turn around and stomp away, and Foley quickly followed, looking over his shoulder one last time. Duane waved at him, and Foley's expression told him how pissed he was.

Duane didn't care.

He stared until he was sure the two had left. That was when Thomas arrived, surrounded by shifter guards. Duane pointed at the spot where Foley and his friend had disappeared, and the guards rushed that way while Thomas stayed back.

"That's Calum?" he asked, tilting his chin toward his chest.

"It is. When Foley attempted to grab him, he was smart enough to shift and fly away." Duane gently lowered his hand, and Calum blinked up at him.

"You did good," Thomas said.

Duane wasn't sure whether he was talking to him or Calum, but it didn't matter. They'd both done well.

"He's going to be a problem, isn't he?" Duane asked.

Thomas sighed. "I'd hoped he wouldn't. We already have more than enough problems with the humans and still not knowing who took a shot at the bobcat alpha. The last thing we need is a war between badgers and bats."

Duane had heard about the bobcat alpha getting shot, but he was surprised that no one knew who had done it. The forest was vast, though, and considering how antagonistic some of the shifter groups were, maybe he shouldn't be.

"There's nothing we can do against Foley?" he asked.

"I'll ask Calder to talk to the bat council member. Hopefully, he'll manage to talk some sense into Foley. I thought the infighting was finally over, but I should have known better. We might have gotten rid of the worst alphas, but that doesn't mean the ones who are left are any nicer."

Duane wanted to help, but as a human, there was nothing he could do. "I'll take Calum inside."

"You do that, and please, check on Kaspar and Julian." Thomas swore again. "I don't like that Foley managed to get to the house. We might need to find a way to close off our territory, or at the very least, get more guards. This is too dangerous."

"I know I was hired to protect your borders with the human world, but if you need anything from me, just let me know." The badgers had welcomed Duane, and he wanted to thank them. He also wanted to keep them and Calum safe, and he was positive he could, at least against Foley.

After picking up Calum's clothes, he left Thomas and walked toward the house. The warmth inside prickled at Duane's skin as soon as he stepped in, and he closed the door so it would stay there. He could hear Kaspar and Julian talking somewhere, but since he wasn't sure Calum wanted them to know what had just happened, he headed toward Calum's bedroom. He doubted Julian and Kaspar hadn't noticed something was happening just outside the door, but Calum needed some time to gather himself.

"I'm going to take you to your bedroom door," he

explained. "You can fly inside from there, and I'll close the door before you shift." Calum would want his privacy, and Duane would give it to him. It was the least he deserved after having to confront Foley again.

Duane wished there was more he could do, but unfortunately, there wasn't. Unless he went out there, snuck into bat territory, and killed Foley, Calum would have to deal with having him in his life, at least for now.

As soon as they were in front of Calum's door, Calum pushed off Duane's chest. Duane made a surprised sound, but Calum didn't give him time to close the door or leave. He shifted back right away, tried his best to ignore the fact that he was completely naked, and threw himself at Duane.

He was done resisting. He was still terrified that Duane would realize he could have so much better, but maybe Julian was right. Maybe Calum should open up and form bonds with people, and not just people he considered family. He hadn't wanted a relationship before, and he wasn't sure he wanted one now, but Duane was here, and Calum liked him.

Once again, Duane had defended him. He was always stepping in when Calum needed him, and Calum was grateful for that, even though he couldn't bring himself to thank Duane for it. He suspected Duane knew how he felt, anyway.

Besides, the two of them had gone on a date. It had gone well, and Calum had hoped they could go on a second one, but that was before all of this had happened. Now, he just wanted Duane, and he hoped Duane wanted him.

Duane's hands landed on Calum's naked hips, making Calum shiver. He pushed closer to Duane, wrapping his arms around Duane's neck and standing up enough to kiss him. Duane came easily, leaning down until Calum could reach him.

The first touch of their lips sent a shiver running down Calum's spine. He'd never been wanton, but then the only person he'd ever been with was Rip. Rip had never allowed Calum to get what he wanted. Even when they had sex, Rip made all the decisions, including what Calum should and shouldn't do and which position he should be in.

A broad hand splayed on the lower part of Calum's back, a fingertip brushing the top of his ass. He tried pulling Duane toward the bed, but Duane didn't move. He was like a rock, and while that made Calum want to climb him and wrap himself around him, he knew why Duane wasn't going along with this.

He leaned back, knowing they needed to talk but not wanting it to happen. That was why he pressed his forehead against Duane's neck, clinging on and praying Duane wouldn't tell him he didn't want this.

"What do you want?" Duane asked.

Calum blinked up at him. "Wasn't it obvious?"

"I'm sure you tried to make it obvious, but knowing you, I'd rather you tell me."

"I don't want to talk," Calum whined.

"I understand, and we don't have to if you're not ready for it. Are you sure this is what you want, though? I didn't think you liked me that much."

Calum snorted and finally looked up at Duane. "Then you don't have eyes. I've liked you since that day at the grocery store and even more after you moved in with us. How could I not? You're everything I could have hoped for in a man, so much that sometimes, I still wonder if you're real."

Duane smiled. "I'm very real, and I want you. As long as you know I won't force you into anything or make demands you're not prepared to meet, we can do whatever you're ready for."

Calum reached around Duane and slammed the door shut,

something he should have done much sooner. Then he pushed Duane against it.

It was odd for Calum to be naked while Duane was completely dressed, but it made him more aroused. It was almost as if what they were doing was illicit, but it wasn't. They were two adults, and neither of them was dating someone else. They could do whatever they wanted, and while Calum wasn't entirely sure what he was ready for, he knew he wanted Duane.

So he reached between them and quickly undid Duane's jeans. Duane didn't move, but Calum could feel his gaze on him. It weighed on his shoulders, but in the best of ways.

He believed Duane when he said he wouldn't force Calum into anything he didn't want. Duane was nothing like Rip, and since they'd started living together, Calum had realized that his relationship with Rip had been borderline abusive, if not outright so. Rip had never cared what Calum wanted, and he'd manipulated him into saying yes to things he didn't want to do.

Duane was the opposite. If Calum stepped away now, he wouldn't try to pull him back. He'd ask him if he was okay, if he needed anything, then he'd leave if that was what Calum wanted.

Calum didn't know how he'd gotten so lucky, but he had, and he was done wasting time or risking Duane meeting someone else. Duane was his, dammit.

He pushed his hand into Duane's jeans and took out Duane's cock. Duane was hard, but then so was Calum. Duane's cock was bigger, though. The skin was smooth and pulsed into Calum's hand as if welcoming him.

Calum didn't have a lot of experience. He could drop to his knees and suck Duane off or drag him toward the bed and present him with his ass. Those were things Rip had liked, but Calum needed to be closer to Duane, at least this time. He wanted skin-to-skin contact, so, letting go of Duane's cock, he scrambled to take off Duane's sweater.

Thankfully, Duane realized what he was doing and helped.

That was all the patience Calum had. As soon as Duane's chest was naked, he wrapped his arms around Duane's neck again. Duane caught him at the hips, but his hands didn't stay there. They slipped lower, cupped Calum's ass, and pulled upward.

It only took a little help for Calum to be in Duane's arms. Duane turned them around, pressing Calum's back against the cool wood of the door. The contact made Calum hiss, but Duane kissed him again, and Calum forgot all about the cold and anything that wasn't Duane. Besides, Duane was warming him up from the inside out.

Calum hooked his legs around Duane's waist. Their cocks slotted together as Duane stepped forward, pressing Calum against the door so hard that Calum wondered if he'd be able to breathe. Duane was careful, though. He kept looking at Calum as if to make sure he was comfortable, and Calum suspected that was precisely what he was doing. Rip had never done anything like that, but Calum needed to stop comparing the two. Rip had also never cared about Calum, but the same couldn't be said when it came to Duane.

He cared. Calum was sure of it.

When Duane thrust his hips forward, Calum whined loudly. The friction was maddening, and it had been so long since he'd had someone else's hands on him that every sensation was overwhelming. He could feel the hair on Duane's chest prickle his own skin, the length and warmth of Duane's cock rubbing against his, the strength making Duane's thighs bulge. Duane was strong enough to hold Calum up and pressed against the door, and Calum never wanted it to end.

Unfortunately, it did way too soon.

Warmth flooded Calum's groin, and he cried out. When

Duane pushed a hand between them and wrapped his fingers around their cocks, he knew he was done. He bit his lower lip so he wouldn't scream and alarm Julian and Kaspar, and when he came, he buried his face against Duane's neck. Duane didn't stop moving until he came, too, the warmth of his spend mixing with Calum's.

Calum sucked in a breath. "Thank you," he murmured.

"You don't have anything to thank me for."

Calum was sure about that. "I feel like I always have something to thank you for. Thank you for not treating me as if I'm fragile. Thank you for giving me this, and so much more."

Duane kissed the side of Calum's head. "Whatever you need from me."

And for the first time, Calum could convince himself that Duane wasn't lying.

CHAPTER TEN

Calum wished he could say that after he and Duane had sex against his bedroom door, things were going smoothly between them. He *wanted* them to go smoothly, but the problem was that he was himself. He could never do anything smoothly, and clearly that included having a relationship.

Was that even what he and Duane had? They'd gone on one date, had sex once, and Calum had been avoiding Duane since then. That day, he'd told himself that he was finally ready for more, that he believed Duane cared about him and wasn't going to leave, and he still believed those things. Once the heat of the moment had passed, it had been harder to ignore how vulnerable he'd made himself when it came to Duane.

He didn't believe Duane would do anything with what he knew. He wasn't the kind of person who would take advantage of Calum's vulnerability the way Rip would have—and had. No, that wasn't the reason Calum was avoiding Duane.

He'd been avoiding Duane because he didn't know *how* to be vulnerable. He'd been vulnerable with Rip, and Rip had taken advantage of that. It was hard to let go now. It was also easier for him to avoid Duane than talk to him, especially with a newborn in the house and Julian about to give birth. Besides, Duane took his job seriously, and with Foley sneaking into badger territory and reaching the house, everyone was on high alert, even Calum, who wouldn't be able to fight his way out of a wet paper bag even if someone ripped it open for him.

Calum was starting to think he'd never feel safe again. He was supposed to be safe in badger territory, but what was he supposed to do if Foley could reach him here? Now, every noise made him jump. Foley had never been inside the house, but it was easy to imagine him breaking a window or opening the door and walking in. This was badger territory. No one locked their door, not even Kaspar and Julian.

That was why, when Calum heard something fall in the kitchen, he swallowed and wondered if he should check what it was. As far as he knew, the baby was asleep, which meant Kaspar was, too. Duane was at work, which only left Julian. He was supposed to be resting, but it would be just like him to try washing the dishes or getting dinner ready.

Calum frowned and rose from the couch. If Julian was in the kitchen cooking, Calum would need to yell at him. Even Cynthia had said Julian needed rest, but Julian didn't seem to understand those words. Every time someone said them to him, he pointed out that he'd been all alone in the forest the first time around and hadn't had time for rest.

That was when Calum pointed out that Julian had been twenty years younger back then.

Calum snickered at the memory of Julian's expression when he'd said that. At least Julian had admitted it was true and that he could probably do with more rest. Still, it was still hard for him to sit and do nothing, which was why Calum wasn't surprised to walk into the kitchen and find him at the stove.

"What are you doing on your feet?" he asked, putting his hands on his hips and glaring.

Julian looked sheepish. "I just wanted to make a cup of tea."

The kettle was full of water, but Julian hadn't turned it on yet. "You could use the microwave."

Julian looked offended at the suggestion. "No one should use the microwave to make tea."

"I didn't take you for a snob. Come on. Let me walk you back upstairs, and I'll bring you your cup of tea once it's ready."

Calum moved to Julian, noticing when he winced. It gave Calum pause, and he wondered what was happening.

It was easy to guess, wasn't it? "When did it start?"

"A few hours ago. It's nothing yet."

"Were you listening when Cynthia said that since it's your second child, labor should be faster?" Calum hoped that would be true. After seeing Kaspar in pain for so many hours, he didn't want the same to happen to Julian.

Why was childbirth so painful? It didn't make sense, since it was necessary for the survival of the species. Who in their right mind would want to have a second child after the pain of birthing the first one?

Well, Calum supposed Julian was one of those people. He'd probably forgotten how painful giving birth to Kari had been, considering it had been more than twenty years ago.

"I'll take you back upstairs," he said firmly. "You can walk up and down the hallway if you need to be on your feet, but I want you close to the bed. I'll bring you your tea, and I'll call Cynthia."

"Thank you." Julian appeared relieved.

"I'll also take care of Cal while Kaspar focuses on you."

"You don't have to do that."

"Maybe not, but I want to do it." Calum hadn't spent a lot of time taking care of the baby. That was Kaspar and Julian's job, while Calum focused on everything else, like keeping the house clean and cooking for everyone. That meant that Julian and Kaspar had the time to bond with their child, rest as much as possible, and enjoy being a family.

Sometimes, looking at them made Calum wonder what his

life would be like if he and Duane had a child. That wasn't enough for him to change his mind when it came to having children, but it was an odd feeling.

"I'm home," someone called out from the entrance.

Calum heard the door close, then the sound of someone moving closer. He recognized Duane's voice, so he wasn't worried.

"What's going on?" Duane asked when he stepped into the kitchen. His gaze went from Julian to Calum. "Is everything okay?"

"Everything is fine. Julian is in labor, which means we'll have a new baby in the house in a few hours."

Julian snorted. "Probably longer."

"You don't know that. Remember, Cynthia said it would be faster."

"I won't be that lucky," Julian grumbled.

Calum was still holding him up, and he felt when the next contraction hit. Julian's stomach went rock hard, and his body tensed. They waited it out with Julian leaning against Calum, breathing in and out as deeply as he could.

Once Calum was sure the contraction was over, he looked up, ready to take Julian upstairs. Duane was still standing there, staring at them with wide eyes, and Calum wondered what was up with him. "I need to take him upstairs. He wanted a cup of tea, so it would be great if you could make it for him. Or you could walk him upstairs, and I'll take care of the tea."

Duane swallowed loudly. "He's about to give birth."

Calum had no idea where Duane was going with this. "Yes. That's the only way to get that baby out of his body."

"He's a guy, with all the guy parts I also have, but he's about to give birth," Duane croaked.

Calum understood what the problem was now, and he rolled his eyes. "Unless you somehow misplaced your eyes, you can't have missed that Julian was heavily pregnant when you moved in. Why is him giving birth a surprise?"

Duane shook his head, seemingly unable to answer. However, Calum had work to do, and that didn't include babysitting Duane. Either the human wrapped his mind around what was happening and helped, or he got out of the way.

Calum didn't care which, as long as he could take care of Julian.

Logically, Duane had known Julian would give birth. It was impossible to ignore, with Julian's stomach making him look like he'd swallowed an entire watermelon—and not one of the small ones. The fact that Julian would have to give birth had been easy to ignore, though. It wasn't any longer, and Duane had no idea what he was supposed to do. What was his job in this situation?

"What do I do?" he asked.

Calum sighed as if he'd asked a stupid question. Duane supposed he had, but he wished Calum would give him a break. He'd only found out about carriers recently.

"Please, make Julian some tea. He wanted a cup, but I want to take him back upstairs," Calum said slowly, as if otherwise, Duane wouldn't understand what he was saying. "As soon as he's in his bedroom, I'll call the healer."

Duane could do that, or at least, he hoped so. Julian was particular about many things, like line drying his clothing and his tea. He'd told Duane it was because for so many years, he had to make do with what he had. He was used to doing things his way, and getting used to having a dryer and using an electric kettle to make tea wasn't easy.

Calum and Julian disappeared. Duane waited a moment longer, and when he could hear them climbing up the steps, he turned to the kettle. Julian had already filled it with water, so it was easy to turn it on and grab a mug and one of the tea packets Julian kept in the cupboards. By the time the water was boiling, Duane had the mug ready, and he poured the water inside, filling three-quarters of the mug.

"I wasn't sure you'd heard me," Calum said as he walked back.

"I guess I'm a bit in shock. Being in the same house as someone giving birth isn't something that happens every day."

Calum grinned. "Unless you live with Kaspar and Julian."

"I've never had to deal with newborns or pregnant people." Several of Duane's friends had had children, but most of the time, they'd been on missions. When they weren't, it was easier and better for everyone to give the new parents space. Duane had no idea how to deal with kids, although he thought he'd been doing pretty well with Cal.

"Then you're getting a crash course. I already called Cynthia, and she'll be here as soon as possible. In the meantime, she wants us to make Julian as comfortable as possible."

"We can do that."

"I sure hope we can. Giving birth isn't a cakewalk."

"Is that something you've been thinking about?"

Calum looked horrified. "Having children? Nope, it's not for me."

Duane was relieved. He wasn't sure where he and Calum stood, since Calum had been avoiding him again, but eventually they'd have to talk about the future and what they were doing.

Duane had been happy to give Calum space, though. They'd gone on one date and had sex once, and it was clear it had been overwhelming for Calum. Duane wanted him to know he wouldn't push him into anything and that they could move at his pace. Giving him space had hopefully shown him that.

But Duane did imagine a future with Calum, and knowing they were on the same track when it came to having children was a good thing. Not that they couldn't change their mind, but Duane hadn't, even though he was almost forty. Calum was quite a bit younger than him, so he might decide it was time to have children in ten years. They'd deal with that, if they were still together.

For a while, everything was a mess. Julian was walking up and down the hallway upstairs, Kaspar by his side. Calum had called Kari, and the man looked both happy and terrified. He kept trying to help his father, then getting flustered and stepping away. The baby was awake, and Calum was juggling him and making phone calls to tell more people that Julian was in labor. After watching him trying to feed Cal while talking on the phone, Duane decided to step in. He'd disliked feeling useless, anyway, and he wanted to help.

He gestured at the baby, then at himself, and opened his arms. Calum was hesitant, but he also looked relieved, which told Duane his offer was welcome. He gently took the baby, settled him into his arms, then grabbed the bottle.

Before coming here, he'd never held a newborn. It had been terrifying, and it still was, but he was getting used to it. Besides, he liked Cal. The baby didn't cry often. He wasn't awake often, though, so that would probably change, but for now, Duane enjoyed the time they spent together, usually during Cal's feedings. Duane had gotten up a few times during the night, and he'd fed Cal even more often during the day, when everyone else was either busy or napping.

He liked that he could be useful. He was a guard, and he went to work every day he was scheduled to, but it felt like he wasn't helping enough at home. Julian, Kaspar, and Calum had welcomed him. Hell, Julian had actually asked him to move in. Ostensibly that was to be Calum's fake boyfriend, but Duane had realized there was probably more to it. He suspected Julian had been playing matchmaker, and he didn't think he was wrong.

A knock on the door made him hesitate. He didn't think the others had heard it, and since he hadn't sat down yet, he didn't have a problem opening. He made his way downstairs, Cal eagerly sucking on his bottle.

When Duane opened the door with his elbow, Cynthia appeared impressed. "You look good with a baby in your arms," she said.

"I don't know about that, but he was hungry. Everyone is upstairs."

She nodded and walked in, carrying her bag like the last time she'd been here to check on Kaspar and Cal. "Ever thought about having your own kids?" she asked. "Or did you leave them behind when you took this job?"

"No kids or significant other, and no. I don't think that having children is for me."

"Really? Well, that's a pity, although I can certainly understand. I didn't have kids, either."

"Too busy taking care of the other kids in the cete?"

She laughed. "Something like that. Now, you said everyone is upstairs?"

"They are, and you know the way. I need to finish feeding this little guy."

"I'll leave you to it."

Duane could hardly believe that by the end of the day, there would be another baby in the house. Things hadn't been easy with Cal, but they'd run smoothly with four adults to take care of him. He wondered if adding a second newborn to the equation would make things more complicated. They'd deal with it, though. It was what they'd been doing since Cal had been born, and even though he wasn't sure it was true, Duane felt like he was part of the family. Julian and Kaspar were always happy to have him take care of Cal, which told

Duane they trusted him.

He liked that.

Calum hadn't meant to listen to Cynthia and Duane's conversation. He'd been coming downstairs to greet the healer and was stunned to hear Duane tell her that he wasn't planning on having children.

Why not?

Calum knew why *he* didn't want kids. He couldn't get over the horror of the pregnancy and childbirth, and even though Cal was cute as a button, that wasn't enough for Calum to want one of his own. He'd seen what Julian and Kaspar had gone through, what their bodies had been put through. Besides, he was more than just a carrier.

He supposed things were different when you were with someone you loved. Kaspar and Julian didn't have a problem with having kids, but they knew the other considered them more than a baby-making machine. Not everyone was like Foley and the other assholes in the forest who thought carriers were incubators, and that included Duane. He'd never force Calum to do anything, but knowing that wasn't enough for Calum to want children with him.

Maybe eventually things would be different. Calum was only twenty-one, and he knew how easy it was to change his mind. It didn't feel like this was something he *would* change his mind on, but who knew what the future would be like for him and Duane? Hell, he couldn't even know if Duane would be there with him.

Still, he hoped that Duane not wanting children meant that they could work as a couple. Of course, to be sure of that, Calum would have to talk to Duane, and he would.

Eventually.

He plastered a smile on his face and finished coming down

the stairs. Both Cynthia and Duane looked up at him, and their smiles were almost identical. They seemed happy to see Calum, which Calum still didn't fully understand.

"He's upstairs," he told Cynthia.

"Duane told me. How far is he?"

"He keeps saying there's time, but the contractions are close." Close enough that after going through this with Kaspar, Calum suspected it wouldn't be long. Either second births really were faster, or Julian had been hiding that he was in labor for a while.

But just like with Kaspar, the next few hours were a game of waiting and listening to the sounds coming from upstairs. Calum and Duane were happy to stay downstairs with the baby, letting Cynthia, Kari, and Kaspar handle everything that was happening upstairs. Eventually, they'd go there, too, but for now, Calum was fine where he was.

He looked at Duane, who was on the couch with Cal on his chest. The baby was asleep, no doubt feeling safe and comfortable. Calum would, too, if he were sleeping on Duane's chest.

He kind of wished that he and Duane had had sex in the evening instead of in the middle of the day. He could have pulled Duane into his bed and slept with him. Instead, he didn't know how sleeping with Duane felt yet, and he wasn't sure when he'd find out. It wouldn't be long, if he talked to Duane.

He cleared his throat, grabbing his courage with two hands, but he still couldn't make the right words come out. Instead, he asked, "I heard you and Cynthia talking. You really don't want kids?"

Duane shook his head. "I feel I'm too old to have children, to be honest."

He was quite a bit older than Calum, but Calum didn't care. "You're not even forty. Besides, you wouldn't be the one carrying the child."

The way Duane looked at Calum made Calum wonder if Duane was imagining him carrying *his* child. A shiver ran down his spine, but he wasn't sure if it was of horror or something else.

"That's true, but still. It's a lot to take on, and I don't imagine it gets easier as you age."

"You look like you're fine with it," Calum said, tilting his chin toward the sleeping baby.

Duane gently patted Cal's butt. "Well, it's easier when you know you can hand the baby over to his parents once you're done with him. I mean, he's cute, and sometimes, I wonder what it would be like to have my own kids, but I don't feel a need for them, you know? What about you? Do you want kids?"

Calum shook his head. "I'm more than just a carrier."

Duane quirked a brow. "I'm very much aware of that. I wasn't saying that you'd have to carry your baby. For all I know, you're bisexual and could meet a woman tomorrow."

Calum couldn't even imagine himself with a woman, although if he was honest, he couldn't imagine himself with anyone who wasn't Duane. "I'm not into women that way. I also don't want to get pregnant. Have you seen what Julian is going through? I don't understand how someone can willingly put themselves through that."

"I can't say I understand, but he and Kaspar seem happy."

Just then, a louder scream made both of them jump. Cal whimpered, but Duane was right there with him, soothing him with a hand on his back. The baby went back to sleep, and Calum got to his feet. He was going upstairs to ask how Julian was doing, but he didn't even reach the stairs when the sweetest sound he'd ever heard reached his ears.

A baby crying.

He turned to look at Duane, who was grinning like a loon.

"She's here," Calum said.

They waited downstairs for another fifteen minutes to give the fathers time to bond with the newborn and Cynthia time to take care of Julian. As soon as she appeared, Calum climbed the stairs two by two. Duane was behind him, carrying Cal, who'd meet his sister while asleep. Neither of them would remember this, anyway.

The bedroom door was open, and when Calum peeked through, he found Kaspar and Julian both in bed. The baby was on Julian's chest, and he was cooing at her. They both looked up when they heard Calum, and they smiled simultaneously. Kari was slumped in an armchair in the corner, looking like he was the one who'd just given birth.

"We brought Cal," Calum said. He suddenly felt awkward, but not as much as he had when Cal had been born.

No matter how hard it was to believe, Julian and Kaspar cared about him. They considered him family, which meant he had a place in their life and in this bedroom right now.

He and Duane tiptoed into the room. Duane gently transferred Cal to Kaspar's chest, then took a step back. He made to leave the room, but Calum grabbed his hand. He didn't look at Duane as he linked their fingers together. He wasn't sure how Duane would react, but thankfully, Duane stayed where he was instead of leaving.

"What's her name?" Duane asked.

Julian and Kaspar looked at each other. "We went with Talia," Kaspar said.

"That's a gorgeous name," Duane murmured.

Calum leaned against Duane and sighed. He wasn't surprised when Duane wrapped an arm around his shoulders and pulled him even closer. Calum might not know where they stood, but he was sure that Duane cared about him, and he cared about Duane. That made Duane family, too, although Calum suspected Julian and Kaspar had considered him that even before he and Calum got together.

But Duane belonged with them. Knowing that made Calum realize how stupid he'd been to push Duane away. It didn't matter that he'd shown Duane how vulnerable he was. Duane cared, and it was time for Calum to give in and allow himself to be happy. No matter what challenges would face them in the future, Calum would always be able to count on Duane and Kaspar and Julian.

In the end, that was all that mattered.

CHAPTER ELEVEN

Calum jerked awake. He was used to it by now, so he started climbing out of his bed before he even realized he could hear one of the babies crying. If he didn't hurry, whoever it was would wake the other, and then, he'd have two crying babies on his hands. He'd have to wake someone, and he didn't want to do that. Everyone else in the house could use more rest. He could, too, but someone needed to get up, and it might as well be him.

Calum reached the nursery too late. Julian was already in the chair by the window, nursing his daughter. Or at least, Calum thought it was Talia. In the darkness, he couldn't tell, and both Julian and Kaspar fed both kids.

Julian looked up when he heard Calum, and his smile was so satisfied and happy that it made something in Calum settle but also yearn.

"I have her if you want to go back to bed," Julian murmured.

"Do you mind if I sit with you for a moment?" Calum didn't want to be alone again right away.

"Of course not."

Calum sat on the floor by the door, leaning his back against the wall. He watched as Julian fed his child, and even though having children wasn't in the cards for him, and he was fine with that, he wanted the happiness that made Julian glow.

"How are things going between you and Duane?" Julian asked.

"I'm not sure."

"You stopped avoiding him?"

Calum wasn't surprised that Julian had noticed that. "I think so."

"Good. You deserve a chance at love and happiness, and Duane is a good man. He'll give that to you and protect and cherish you for as long as you allow him to."

Julian sounded convinced of that, and Calum agreed. He'd been watching Duane, half expecting him to change his mind about them, but he hadn't so far, and Calum didn't think he would. Besides, it wasn't just about him. It was enough to watch Duane with the babies or with Kaspar and Julian. His behavior with them had shown that he was a nice and caring man, and what more could Calum want?

"I'm scared," he confessed.

Julian didn't seem surprised. "I think everyone would be scared in your place. Considering what your alpha did to you, what he continues doing to you, and how your first relationship ended, it's normal to be hesitant. I think Duane will be good for you, though."

"How do you figure that?"

"You've been more open and welcoming since he arrived. I'm not saying you're friendly with people you don't know and trust, but you're no longer biting people's heads off, which is a relief."

Calum chuckled. "I wasn't that bad."

Julian's expression was serious. "You were. You kept everyone away, even Kaspar and me, in some ways. We didn't think you'd ever fully open up to anyone, and we certainly didn't expect you to fall for a human, but maybe that's what you needed."

"Why?"

"Duane didn't know about carriers before he arrived in the forest. He doesn't expect you to have his child and won't demand it of you. A shifter might have, but not him, and you need that."

"I need someone who respects me."

"Exactly, and he does. As long as you give both him and yourself a chance, I think things for the two of you will be great. I'm not looking forward to when you decide you need your own space and move out, but we'll deal with it, because it will mean you're happy. There's nothing more Kaspar and I want for you."

"I'll still help with the babies." Although Calum didn't believe moving out was anywhere in his near future.

Julian shook his head. "That's not why Kaspar and I aren't looking forward to it. It's because we love you and enjoy living with you. Things are slightly different for Kaspar because he's younger, but in the time you've been here, I've started seeing you as another son. It's always sad when your children leave the nest, but it's also a happy moment because it means they're living their life."

And Calum *wanted* to live his life. Talking with Julian and thinking about how things with Duane were going had made him realize he'd been hiding from life. It had been easier than dealing with the possible heartbreak and pain, but it also meant he was missing out on a lot. He didn't want children, but he could have a relationship, a home, and even a job. Hell, Cynthia had hinted at the fact that she wouldn't mind if he wanted to be her apprentice. It was too soon for Calum to say yes, but maybe he would in the future.

He got to his feet. "I'll go back to bed," he murmured.

"I'll see you tomorrow. It's good to finally have you with us, Calum."

And it was good to be here. What Calum had gone through hadn't been as bad as what the other carriers had endured, but it didn't mean it wasn't bad. Calum was learning to deal with his past—to let go of the pain and trust his future.

That was why, instead of going back to his bedroom, he

stopped in front of Duane's door. He knocked, but he wasn't surprised when Duane didn't answer. He hesitated, then decided he might as well take a leap and opened the door.

Duane was star-fished in the middle of his mattress, on his stomach. The blankets were twisted around his legs, but his chest was bare, and Calum could see all of it thanks to the light streaming in from the window. He couldn't see colors, but he didn't need to. He already knew Duane. He knew what Duane looked and *felt* like, but he wanted more.

He closed the door and stepped toward the bed. He was nervous, but he took off his t-shirt and dropped it to the floor. His pants were next, until he was only wearing boxer briefs like Duane. Then he knelt on the bed and crawled closer. He put a hand on Duane's shoulder, expecting to need at least a few moments to wake him up, but Duane reacted instantly. He twisted and rolled to his back, grabbing Calum's wrist as he went. Calum ended up on top of him, the breath whooshing out of his lungs. His eyes were wide as he stared at Duane, and Duane stared back.

"Calum?" Duane asked, sounding confused.

Calum nodded. "It's me."

"What are you doing here? Has something happened?"

Calum shook his head. "Not really. I just needed to be with you." Then Calum kissed Duane.

He didn't need them to talk. They could do so tomorrow morning when they woke up together in Duane's bed. It wasn't the time for words.

It was time for them to be together.

For a moment, Duane didn't react, not even to kiss Calum back. It was enough to make Calum hesitate, and he dropped back against the pillow as he wondered if he'd just made a huge mistake. Duane didn't let him go far, though. When he felt Calum move away, he pushed a hand under Calum's upper back and cupped the back of his head, holding him in place as he finally kissed him.

It was everything Calum could have wanted. He was nervous, which made sense since the only person he'd ever had sex with was Rip, but Rip was the past, while Duane was the future. Calum trusted him.

"What do you want?" Duane murmured as he kissed down Calum's neck.

Rip had never done anything like that. Calum hadn't realized it at the time, but only Rip's pleasure mattered when they were together. He'd always been at the center of everything, including sex, and Calum had gone along with it because he hadn't wanted Rip to break up with him. In hindsight, it had been stupid and he'd have been better off on his own, but he hadn't known it then.

He did now.

"You," he murmured.

Duane grinned. He'd slid down Calum's body and was kissing Calum's collarbone, but he looked up at him now. "You already have me. I was looking for a more detailed explanation."

But Calum didn't have the words to explain. He stared at Duane as Duane's smile slipped, but thankfully, Duane seemed to understand. He rose on his knees and kissed Calum's forehead as he reached sideways toward his nightstand. Calum didn't understand for a moment, but he did when he saw Duane take out a bottle, and even in the darkness, he knew what it was. He felt his cheeks heat, but they would need it for the next step.

"Okay?" Duane asked as he raised the tube.

Calum nodded. Duane was smiling again, and he didn't hesitate to drop the lube and help Calum take off his boxer briefs. He went exquisitely slow, dragging the fabric over Calum's thighs, carefully avoiding his cock even though it was the one spot Calum wanted him to touch.

So when Duane finally pulled the briefs off Calum's feet and reached for his own, Calum let his knees fall to the side, exposing himself. Duane paused and took a moment to look at Calum in a way that made Calum want to hide.

Calum knew what Duane was seeing. He was pale and had long legs, maybe too long. That didn't seem to bother Duane, though, because he leaned down and kissed his way up Calum's right leg. Calum giggled when Duane paused at his knee to lick there, then again when he stopped where his thigh met his groin. He'd never realized he was so sensitive in those spots.

He felt like Duane was exploring him and helping him discover new things about himself, but it felt like too much. He wasn't sure he could stand it, especially not this time. He wanted to lose himself in Duane, but that wouldn't happen if Duane spent so much time on Calum.

Hoping he wasn't making a mistake, Calum grabbed his arm and looked at the tube of lube that had landed next to him. Duane laughed and finally grabbed the lube, clearly having gotten the hint.

"You're bossy," he murmured as he slicked his fingers.

"Only when I know what I want."

"And you want me?"

Calum nodded. He'd never wanted anyone the way he wanted Duane, not even Rip. All these feelings confused him and made him feel like his chest was about to explode. It was easier to focus on what Duane was doing to his body.

Duane pushed his slicked fingers along the crack of Calum's ass. Calum held his breath as Duane rubbed small circles around his hole before pushing in one finger. With Rip, that had been Calum's job, and it was odd to have someone else do it.

Not that Calum was going to protest. Duane made him feel like he mattered, and he could let go without being afraid of getting hurt.

Duane added another finger. Calum made a strangled sound and wriggled his butt, wanting both more and less. Sex had never been like this with Rip. It had never been so intimate and just *good*. Calum couldn't imagine it being like this with anyone but Duane.

Duane tugged on Calum's balls with his free hand, then rolled them, making Calum writhe. Calum had played with himself, but it had never felt like this. Duane seemed to be able to do what Calum liked and needed without even asking, which puzzled Calum in the best of ways.

"Calum?" Duane asked.

Calum had closed his eyes, wanting to enjoy this moment as fully as he could. He blinked them open now, enjoying the sight of Duane leaning over him. Duane's cock brushed against Calum's thigh, sending a shiver down his spine. He could feel that Duane was wearing a condom, and he hadn't even had to ask. "Yes?"

"Ready?"

"Yeah," Calum croaked.

Duane stared at him for a moment, but he didn't ask if he was sure. Instead, he slid his fingers out of Calum's body, lifted his knees, and slid his arms under them. He moved forward, bringing Calum's lower body up until Calum could feel the head of his cock slide against his crack.

Calum sucked in a breath. He was ready.

Duane pushed in slowly but steadily, and Calum didn't miss the fact that he was looking at the spot where their bodies were joined. The thought of what Duane was seeing made Calum shudder, and he wished he could see it, too, although it made him feel strange. Calum gasped, and Duane stopped instantly, staring at him.

"I'm fine," Calum reassured him. "It's just a lot."

"We can stop or take it even more slowly."

"No. I want you."

Duane's smile was soft. "And you have me." He pushed until their bodies were flush together. He arched his back, groaning, incapable of keeping the sounds in.

"That's . . . yeah. That's what I wanted."

Duane leaned forward. "Good. Whatever you want, I'll give it to you. You're mine, Calum."

And Calum was more than okay with that.

Duane had been stunned to find Calum in his bedroom, but this had been brewing between them for a while now, so maybe he shouldn't have been. He hadn't thought Calum could open himself up enough to allow Duane to make love to him.

But he had, and Duane wanted to give him everything.

He rocked back and forth, staring as Calum's body undulated under him. Calum had a surprised expression, as if he didn't expect this to be pleasurable. Knowing what he did about Calum's ex-boyfriend, Duane wasn't surprised, even though he wanted to find the man and wring his neck for not treating Calum right. Duane supposed that Rip's loss was his gain, though. Calum was his now, and he'd treat him the way he ought to be treated.

He leaned back and pushed Calum's knees further apart so he could thrust faster. The headboard slammed against the wall, and Duane froze.

Calum laughed. "There's nothing on that side. Besides, I'm pretty sure Julian knows what we're doing. We talked in the nursery."

"Doesn't mean I want to bother him and Kaspar."

"You won't."

Calum seemed convinced of that, and Duane decided to trust him. Calum tightened around him, urging him to start moving again, so he did. He wanted to give Calum what he'd come looking for.

For several moments, Calum stayed passive, as if he wasn't sure what to do. Then he thrust down and tightened around Duane as Duane pushed into him. His eyes widened, and his lips parted on a silent cry.

Calum had broken the dam. His cheeks flushed and he moved, awkwardly at first, then with more confidence. He knew what he wanted, and he was taking it. Duane had never seen anything so sexy.

Duane's orgasm took him by surprise. He groaned and squeezed his eyes shut, but hands on his arms made them snap open. He looked down as Calum pulled him toward him, and he was happy to go.

They kissed, Calum's hands in Duane's short hair, pulling him close. Duane felt Calum try to roll them, but there was no way he'd be able to move Duane unless Duane helped.

Which he happily did.

Duane rolled them so he was on his back with Calum straddling him. His legs dangled off the bed, but he didn't care because he couldn't look away from Calum riding him. He'd been shy and hesitant before, but now, he was taking his pleasure, and it was almost enough to make Duane hard again.

He wasn't completely soft, but Calum still needed to come, so Duane took advantage of their new position and wrapped a hand around Calum's cock.

He loved the way Calum moaned in answer. His cock jerked in Duane's hand, and Duane focused on Calum's pleasure as Calum moved on top of him.

Suddenly Calum stopped moving. His body tensed, and his cock spurted all over Duane's hand and stomach. Duane stroked him through it, feeling satisfied in a way he hadn't in years, if ever.

He hadn't expected to find love when he'd decided to move to the forest. He'd wanted to help, and he was, but Calum was giving him a chance at a life he'd known he wanted but hadn't thought he'd have. As Calum lowered down and rested his cheek on Duane's chest, Duane knew this was it for him. His life was here, with Calum.

Moving to the forest was the best thing he'd ever done.

CHAPTER TWELVE

Duane stared beyond the fence. From where he was, he could hear people chanting. He was glad he couldn't hear what they were saying. It was nothing good, and he didn't have patience for what those assholes thought about shifters.

He wouldn't have had the patience even if he and Calum weren't together, but they were. Duane hated that some people thought Calum shouldn't have equal rights just because he could turn into a bat. He understood why some humans were afraid of shifters, but there was nothing scary about most of them.

Duane had no doubt that some shifters were dangerous, but then so were some humans. They might not be able to shift into animals, but it didn't mean they weren't predators. Most humans didn't realize that, or if they did, they ignored it. Duane knew why.

It was easier not to deal with it if it didn't impact them personally.

But all of this impacted *Duane's* life. He'd seen with his own two eyes that shifters were just like everyone else and wanted pretty much the same things. They wished for a home, a family, and happiness. Some of them found that in the forest, but others yearned for more. Duane couldn't berate them for that, but he could berate the humans chanting by the gate that shifters were nothing more than animals.

Dammit. He *could* hear what they were saying.

"I would've thought that getting a boyfriend would make

you happy," Saul said.

He and Duane had been assigned the same shift and the same area of the fence. They always went out in teams in case something happened. It helped time pass, too, for which Duane was grateful. "What are you talking about?"

Saul gestured at Duane's face. "That scowl. Shouldn't you be happy? Or did you and your boyfriend fight already?"

Duane was angry, but not at Saul, and he reminded himself of that. The people who pissed him off were out of reach, yelling their hate by the gate. "He has a name, you know," Duane pointed out.

"I'm aware. You're still grumpy, though."

Duane sighed. "It has nothing to do with Calum. I just can't believe these people."

Saul grimaced. "I can't say I blame you."

Movement beyond the fence made both of them stand up straighter. Duane squinted, trying to see what was happening. He wasn't surprised when two humans burst out from between the trees on the other side of the fence a few seconds later. They looked startled to see Saul and Duane, but unfortunately, it didn't last for long.

"Look, we found two of the animals," one of them said, elbowing the other.

Duane rolled his eyes. Did they really think that way? What were they, six? Clearly, some adults weren't any smarter than children. Hell, Duane was ready to bet that some children were smarter than adults, including these two.

"Someone's coming on our side," Saul said.

That was the last thing they needed. Duane wasn't sure where to look, but thankfully, there were two of them. "Keep an eye on the two assholes on the other side of the fence," he told Saul.

Saul nodded and turned his attention to the fence while Duane moved to face whoever was coming on their side. He didn't have to wait long. A few moments later, two men appeared. He recognized one of them as Dean, a member of Luther's team, but not the other.

He was relieved he wouldn't have to fight on both sides, but he worried about what the humans would do. Duane, Saul, and Dean were human, but something told Duane the other guy wasn't. He hadn't been there when Duane had met Luther's team, but if Duane was lucky, he was a new guard or something.

"How are things going?" Dean asked.

Duane gestured behind himself. "We've had better days, as you can see." He turned his attention to the other guy. He looked to be in his late twenties, maybe early thirties. His messy dark hair made him look like he'd just rolled out of bed, and his dark eyes jumped from Duane to the fence, then back. He was tall, around Duane's six foot three, and he stood close enough to Dean that Duane wondered if there was something between them.

He smiled and nodded. "I don't think we met before. I'm Duane."

The man was now staring at the humans on the other side of the fence. Duane could hear them bickering and trying to get Saul's attention, but everyone was ignoring them.

"I'm Jasper," the man eventually said.

He didn't add details, but Dean did as he rolled his eyes. "He's the skunk alpha."

Duane almost groaned. He could only hope the humans hadn't heard that, but of course, he didn't have that much luck. The two assholes stopped talking for a second, and Duane hoped they were leaving, but he should have known better.

"An alpha?" one of them asked the other.

Duane turned and glared at them. "Leave."

"We don't take orders from animals," asshole one

snapped.

"Then it's good I'm human. I told you to leave, and you're going to do just that."

Asshole two opened his mouth, but a shot rang through the forest before he could say anything. Duane reacted instinctively. One of the humans squeaked and looked around, standing there like an idiot. The other turned and ran away.

Thankfully, Dean had reacted by pushing Jasper toward the trees, but it took Duane a second to realize something was wrong. Jasper was clutching at his shoulder, and blood seeped between his fingers.

"Where did it come from?" Duane asked as he crouched next to the two. Dean was shielding Jasper with his body while at the same time trying to check on the wound. He was pale and his eyes were wide, and since he had training, Duane suspected there was more to the situation than he knew. There had to be a good reason Dean was so frantic.

"I don't know," Dean said. "You were with us. We were talking, and someone shot at Jasper."

"You need to get out of here."

Another shot echoed, the bullet lodging into the trunk of the tree they were next to. Small bits of bark rained over their heads, and since Dean was clearly unable to think right now, Duane had to take matters into his own hands.

He grabbed Dean and forced him to his feet. Dean tried to push him away, but Duane was focused on Jasper. "Can you run?"

Jasper was so pale that Duane wouldn't have been surprised if he'd fainted. Still, the alpha nodded and got up. He wobbled, but Dean was next to him in seconds, wrapping an arm around his waist.

"Did you come to your senses?" Duane asked him.

Dean nodded curtly. "I'll take him to Thomas's house. He'll be safe there."

"Try to stay between the trees. Saul and I will take care of the shooter."

"Get him."

Duane watched them run away, and once he was sure Dean knew what he was doing, he turned to Saul. He could hear people yelling and footsteps coming closer, and he hoped it was the good guys, not the shooter.

He was relieved to see he was right when, seconds later, two other guards appeared. "We heard shots," Sonia said.

"There was an alpha here, and someone shot at him," Duane confirmed.

"Where's the shooter?"

"Whoever it is only shot twice. It came from over there," Duane said, turning.

Fuller nodded. "Go with the alpha, and make sure he's safe. We have this."

Duane was torn. He wanted to find the shooter and make sure they'd never shoot anyone else again, but he also felt he needed to check in on Dean and Jasper, just in case. Besides, the shooter could have taken off after them, and they might need help.

"Saul," Duane said.

Saul followed him deeper into the forest. Duane's brain was working, trying to figure out who the shooter had been. It had seemed to come from inside the forest, but why would a shifter shoot another shifter? Wouldn't they fight it out in their shifted form?

Could the shooter have been hiding on the human side of the forest? Maybe those two assholes had been sent as a distraction. If that was the case, it had worked, and Duane was already berating himself for that. It would make sense for humans to want to shoot at shifters, possibly even to kill them. They'd been chanting that shifters were nothing more than animals for days now, and some of them were hunters.

The thought made Duane feel sick. He had no doubt that given the opportunity, many humans wouldn't have a problem with hunting shifters. As far as he was concerned, it made *them* the monsters, not the shifters, but he didn't know if he hoped that was what happened here. Jasper wasn't just a shifter. He was an alpha, and while things seemed to be smooth enough between the different groups of shifters in the forest, Duane knew that wasn't the case.

So who was behind the shooting? Who had tried to kill Jasper, and why?

Calum wasn't exactly uncomfortable, but he also wasn't fully comfortable. He should be, since he was surrounded by carriers and he'd lived with them for months, but he'd never been close to any of them except for Julian and Kaspar. That was his fault, but it didn't make him feel better as he looked around the room.

Today, the carriers were visiting. There weren't many of them left at the Bishop house, but those who still lived there wanted to meet the babies, and Kaspar and Julian were happy to make that happen. They were all carriers, and they'd stuck together while they lived in the Bishop house. They'd become a kind of family, and the bond between them hadn't faded just because they didn't live together anymore, or at least, that was what Calum thought. He wouldn't know, since he didn't have a bond with any of the visitors in the room.

"They're adorable," Redley cooed.

"Not so much when they wake up at two in the morning," Julian said, but he was smiling.

No matter how tired he was, he always seemed to be smiling. Calum knew it had to do with the fact that he hadn't thought he could have more children after Kari. His pregnancy had been a surprise, coming right after he and Kaspar had decided to try having a child and Kaspar had become pregnant.

"You love it," Hector said.

He was holding Cal, and Calum couldn't help but feel protective of the baby. He wouldn't say Cal was his favorite, but he was his namesake.

Talia was in Julian's arms, with Redley leaning over her and making funny faces. Both babies were awake, which hopefully meant they'd fall asleep together. Things had been overwhelming after Cal was born, but it was nothing next to what had happened when Talia had come into the world. With two babies in the house, there wasn't much sleep to be had, even though the four adults took turns getting up during the night. Calum took his job seriously, which meant he tried to be the one getting up. Kaspar and Julian often got there first, which was understandable, considering the babies were theirs. It was easier if they fed them, but they needed sleep, and that wouldn't happen if they got up every hour.

Because, of course, the babies weren't in sync. When one went to sleep, the other woke up, and if they gave the newly awakened baby time to cry, they'd wake up the other. If there was something worse than one baby crying at night, it was two babies crying.

A phone chirped, and Calum watched Redley lean back to take it out of his pocket. It made Calum's hands itch to check on his, too, and maybe text Duane. He didn't want to be clingy, so he stayed where he was, turning his attention back to the babies.

It didn't last long. Redley gasped, and everyone looked at him.

"Someone was shot at the fence," he said.

Calum felt like he was about to throw up. He got to his feet, but he had nowhere to go. What could he do? "Who?" he croaked.

Redley grimaced. "I don't know. Whoever it was is at Thomas's house now, though."

Calum started to move, then remembered that he was here to help Julian and Kaspar. He turned to look at them, and they both nodded. Julian even gestured at Calum to go, and he didn't have to insist.

Calum ran out.

Redley called out for him, but Calum didn't stop. Duane was at work, which meant he was guarding the fence. Was he the one who'd gotten shot?

Calum couldn't imagine his life without Duane, even though they'd met recently. They'd spent a lot of time together, especially since they'd become a couple, and he thought he'd have years, if not decades, to enjoy the man's company. Was it over already? Calum wouldn't be surprised. He didn't have any luck when it came to relationships, as his past with Rip showed. Duane was different, so maybe Calum would be unlucky in a different way with him.

Maybe he'd lose him.

Calum ran through the forest, headed toward Thomas's house. When he got there, there were people *everywhere*. Three guards stood in front of the house, quietly talking to each other. Calum recognized them because of the uniform, and his stomach sank when he saw that one of the guards was Saul. He didn't know the man well, but Duane had introduced them. He was Duane's usual partner, which meant that where he was, Duane was supposed to be, too.

Yet, he was nowhere to be seen.

The front door was open, and two badger shifters came out. They were part of cete security, and they seemed to have a goal in mind, because they strode away from the house, heading into the forest toward the fence.

Calum needed to see Duane.

He rushed toward the house, ignoring the people calling

out to him to stop. He wouldn't stop until he got to Duane and made sure his boyfriend was fine. Since Duane wasn't outside, he had to be inside.

Calum checked the kitchen first, but there was no one there. He moved toward the living room but never got there because Duane was standing in the hallway, talking to Thomas. Calum cried out and ran toward him, and Duane was just in time to turn and catch him. Calum threw himself into his boyfriend's arms, a sob tearing out of his throat.

"What happened? Are you all right? Are you hurt?" he asked, pushing away from Duane's chest and running his palms over him. If Duane was hurt, Calum would find out.

Duane caught both of Calum's hands and pulled them to his chest. "I'm fine. I wasn't the one who got shot."

It seemed to be true. Calum hadn't found any kind of wound, and while there was blood on Duane's sweater, Calum was pretty sure it didn't belong to him. "Are you sure?"

Duane's expression was soft. "I'm sure. I'd tell you if I was hurt, but there's not even a scratch on me."

Calum breathed more easily now. He leaned against Duane's chest again, letting his boyfriend wrap his arms around him. Duane was safe, which was all that mattered.

Someone cleared their throat, and Calum remembered that Thomas had been talking to Duane when he'd barged in. His cheeks flushed, and he turned to look at the alpha, but he wasn't ready to step away from Duane.

Thomas arched a brow as he looked from Calum to Duane. "Is there something you want to tell me? Or is this still part of the fake boyfriend thing?"

"It's not fake anymore," Calum blurted out. He wanted Thomas to know in case something happened to Duane, though. If Thomas didn't know, he wouldn't think of telling Calum.

Thomas grinned. "That's good to hear. I was hoping something like that would happen."

Now it was Calum's turn to arch a brow. "Were you playing matchmaker again?"

"Possibly. I'm glad to see it worked."

Calum was, too, but even more so that Duane was okay. Who had been shot, though? "Can you tell me what happened?"

"How did you know to come here and that someone was shot?" Thomas asked.

"You know how things go. Redley was visiting, and he got a text that someone was shot at the fence. That was all he knew, though, and I had to come."

"Gossip in this pack," Thomas said, shaking his head. "I swear, everyone behaves like little old ladies who don't have anything better to do with their day."

That might be so, but Calum was glad someone had texted Redley. He wouldn't have known something had happened otherwise.

"Jasper was shot," Thomas continued.

It took Calum a moment to remember who Jasper was. "The skunk alpha?" Jasper was new to it, having taken his father's place. Everyone was happy he had, but him getting shot didn't sound good.

"Yes," Thomas confirmed. "Cynthia is already working on him, but he'll be fine. He got hit in the shoulder."

"Was it the humans?" It would make sense since, apparently, Jasper had been at the fence. Calum never went that way, too afraid of seeing humans on the other side of the fence, but sometimes, when they were very noisy, he could hear them. Besides, he had a TV. The news showed how many people were gathered outside the fence protesting every evening. Thankfully, that hadn't stopped the people from trying to change the laws to allow shifters more freedom, but

Calum couldn't help but wonder if it just meant the humans protesting would try to find another way. They didn't want the laws to be changed and hated shifters.

"I don't believe so," Duane said. "The shots came from our side of the fence. I didn't see much, but I'm almost a hundred percent sure of that." He looked at Thomas. "Who would shoot Jasper, though? I don't know him, but you do."

Thomas pinched the bridge of his nose. He looked tired. "I have no idea, but unfortunately, Jasper isn't the first alpha who's been shot recently."

Duane had been afraid of that. He vaguely remembered someone telling him another alpha had been shot some time ago, but since no one had given him details, he'd thought it had to do with the infighting in the forest. Clearly, Thomas didn't think so.

"No one told me about that," he said.

"Because we didn't think it was relevant. It happened in the forest, which means it couldn't be a human."

"The forest is vast. Someone could have climbed the fence, especially since you didn't have guards until recently. Besides, wouldn't it make more sense for a shifter to attack in their shifted form?"

"It depends on what their goal was. The bobcat alpha was the person who got shot, and for a while, we thought we might lose him. His son had to step up and take his place as alpha, although that's over now."

"You can't know it was the same shooter."

"I can't, but there's no way this is a coincidence."

Duane agreed. As far as he knew, the only people in the forest who had guns were the human guards and Luther's team. It was possible for a shifter to find a gun, but they'd have to move it from the human world into the forest.

Humans weren't eager to arm the shifters, so it would be complicated.

But if it had been a human, how had they gotten in? And why were they shooting alphas? "Is there something in common between the bobcat alpha and Jasper?"

"Not as far as I can think of. They're both alphas, of course, but I don't know about anything else."

"What would have happened if they'd died?"

"As I explained, when it comes to the bobcats, Chris took his father's place until he healed. When it comes to Jasper, though, things are more complicated. He just became alpha, and as far as I know, he doesn't have an heir."

"So there would be no one to take his place?" Duane didn't fully understand how the various groups worked, but that was what made the most sense.

"Someone would eventually. If no one from the skunks stepped forward, the council would choose someone, possibly another kind of shifter. The skunks wouldn't have been left on their own."

"A human might not have known that, but a shifter would have. So if a shifter is trying to kill alphas, why are they doing it?"

"Your guess is as good as mine," Thomas said. "I really thought we were finally on the right track, but clearly, I was wrong. There has to be a reason behind all of this."

The problem was that they didn't know what that reason was.

Duane looked down at Calum, who was still clinging to him. He didn't want to leave, but he had work to do. "I should go back to the fence," he murmured.

"Actually, I want you and Calum to go home," Thomas said.

"I'm not done with my day."

"You were shot at. You helped Jasper get here. You deserve

some rest and perhaps a shower, considering how much blood is on your clothes."

Jasper's blood. Duane might not know the guy, but he'd panicked at the thought that Jasper might die. Nothing like Dean, who'd freaked out until the healer arrived. Duane could tell there was something between those two, but he hadn't said anything. It was none of his business.

"Thank you," he said. "I'll take advantage of that and spend the rest of the day home with Calum." Duane could almost feel Calum retreating now that he was sure Duane was safe. He was still in Duane's arms, but he'd tensed, and Duane knew him by now. Calum was terrified that he'd lose Duane, and he still thought that putting distance between them would help him not feel pain when that happened. Duane fully expected him to try doing just that, but he wouldn't allow it.

Calum was his, and he was Calum's. Nothing would change that. Certainly not a shooter who wasn't even that good.

There was no way Duane would have missed that shot if he'd been the one shooting. He didn't know if it had been on purpose, possibly to blame the humans, or if the shooter just wasn't very good. Still, good or not, he'd managed to wound two alphas. They had to find the guy, but not today.

Duane and Calum left Thomas's house with the promise that Thomas would let them know how Jasper was. They silently walked toward their house, and as they moved, it was even more obvious that Calum was keeping his distance. They weren't holding hands, and Calum was careful to avoid looking at Duane.

That wouldn't do.

Duane stopped in the middle of the path and waited for Calum to realize it. When Calum turned to him, a frown on his face, Duane grabbed his shoulder and pulled him into his arms. Calum squeaked, but thankfully, he didn't push away.

"I'm fine," Duane said, even though he'd already said those words several times. "And I want you to stop this."

"Stop what?"

Calum was rigid in Duane's arms. "Stop retreating. I know it was scary, and I wish you hadn't had to go through it. It can't have been easy to hear that someone by the fence had been shot and not know if it was me. But I'm not going anywhere, Calum. I'm not leaving you, dead or alive."

"You could have been killed." Calum's voice trembled.

"I won't be. You heard Thomas. He doesn't think this was a coincidence, which meant the shooter was targeting Jasper. I'm not an alpha."

"But your job is dangerous."

Duane needed to get through to Calum. "It is, but how would you feel if something happened to me and you've broken up with me? Do you really think that breaking up will help you not feel anything for me? Because it wouldn't work in my case. Whether or not we're together, I'm in love with you. It would hurt either way if I were to lose you." That was why Duane was ready to do anything to ensure that didn't happen.

Calum looked up. "I was terrified," he whispered.

Duane kissed his forehead. "I know, and I understand. We can talk about it if you want me to stop being a guard, although I'm not ready to do that. I'm cautious, though, and I never work alone. I'm as safe as I can be."

But that didn't make him bulletproof. This shooter was after alphas, which meant Duane was safe from him, but what if some of the humans out there decided to do something stupid? Today, two of them had come close enough to the fence that Duane had wondered if they were going to try to climb it. What would happen if someone actually did?

Duane's job was dangerous, even though he wasn't in the

military anymore. He'd known that when he'd accepted it and didn't regret it. Being here had given him Calum, and he was nowhere ready to go and leave him behind.

"I need you to trust me on this," he murmured. "I know what I'm doing. I can't promise nothing will ever happen to me, but even during my years in the military, I was only wounded a handful of times, and never badly. This job is a cakewalk next to what I had to do back then, and I need you to understand that and to understand that no matter how hard you push me away, I'm not going anywhere."

Duane wasn't sure Calum believed him, but he wouldn't have a problem repeating those words again and again until he did.

Because Calum was it for Duane, and he'd always been stubborn. He didn't give up faced with obstacles and challenges, under any circumstance.

He wouldn't give up even if his obstacle in this case was Calum himself.

CHAPTER THIRTEEN

Duane was right. Pulling away from him wouldn't change Calum's feelings, but Calum had done it anyway.

After he and Duane had come home following the shooting a few days ago, Calum had made a beeline for his bedroom. Duane had been disappointed, but Calum hadn't been able to stop himself. How could he, when the only thing he could think of was Duane getting hurt, or worse, killed? He'd needed some time to wrap his mind around what had happened and why he'd freaked out so badly, but the hour or so he'd needed had turned into days, and now he didn't know how to reach out to Duane again.

But he wanted to, so, so much.

His life without Duane wasn't one he enjoyed. He hadn't realized how important Duane had become in his everyday life until now, but he should have. He was falling in love with Duane, after all. That was why he'd thought it would be better to push him away, but now that he'd done it, albeit not intentionally, he could see Duane was right. He was still worried every time Duane left the house. He still wanted to tell him to stay with him and never leave the house again.

But Duane had a life, and from what he'd told Calum, he didn't want to quit his job. It made sense. Duane wanted to protect Calum and the other shifters in the forest, and he was good at it. Calum couldn't demand he leave his job. It would be selfish, and Calum was trying not to be, even though he was terrified.

He just didn't know how to deal with that fear.

How was he supposed to live with the knowledge that something could happen to Duane any second he was out of the house? Duane would be safer here, next to Calum, but it wouldn't be a life either of them wanted. He loved spending time with Duane, but he also enjoyed being alone or with Kaspar and Julian. He couldn't imagine being with Duane all the time, yet at the same time, he wished he could make that happen.

He groaned and pressed his forehead against the cold glass of his bedroom window. He was trying to make sense of his feelings, but he wasn't sure he could. Things had been so much easier when he'd pushed everyone away. He hadn't had to worry about anyone's safety.

But that wasn't true. Even though he'd pushed people away, he'd worried about Julian and Kaspar, the other carriers, and even Thomas. Slowly, day by day, he'd come to care about all of them, even the people he had little contact with. He'd come to see them as his family, his cete, and there was no way out of that. Unless he went deep into the forest and lived alone, he'd always be worried about someone. Hell, at this point, he'd be worried even if he did go and live on his own.

So where did it leave him?

The sound of a baby crying jerked him out of his thoughts. At least he could count on them to make sense, no matter what happened. At their age, there was little they wanted and nothing Calum couldn't provide.

He made his way toward the nursery, but the crying cut out before he could get there. He still peeked in, in case whoever was inside needed help.

Julian was changing Cal, softly talking to him. Calum stared for a moment, trying to understand if seeing Julian with his son made him want children.

The answer to that was still no.

Julian turned as if he heard Calum and smiled. "What are you doing lurking out there?"

"I didn't want to bother you." Calum stepped in.

"You never bother me." His eyes narrowed, but Cal cooed, and Julian turned his attention back to him.

He was an old hand at changing babies, and in moments, Cal was cleaned up and dressed again. It seemed that was all he'd wanted, because he'd stopped crying.

"Are you ready to talk about it?" Julian asked.

Calum didn't even try to tell Julian there was nothing he wanted to talk about. Julian was more a father to him than his own father had ever been, and Calum liked it that way.

He went to stand next to the window while Julian settled in the chair there. Everything was silent for a moment, giving Calum time to gather his thoughts. He wasn't quite sure how to explain how he felt, but he wanted to try, and he was pretty sure it was the first time. Usually, he felt better hiding away, even from Kaspar and Julian. He'd always believed he'd be better off on his own, but he'd come to realize that wasn't the case.

"I pulled away from Duane," he said.

"We noticed. He noticed, too, and he doesn't like it."

"I don't like it, either. I just don't know how to stop myself from freaking out every time he goes to work."

Julian knew about the shooting. Everyone did by now. Calum didn't have to explain, but he wasn't sure Julian fully understood how he'd felt. "When Redley said someone had been shot by the fence, I thought it was Duane," Calum said as he stared at the trees outside the window. "In just a few seconds, I thought I'd lost him. I freaked out."

"But you didn't lose him."

"What if I do? What happens if he gets hurt a week or a month from now? How am I supposed to deal with that?"

"Not on your own. You'll never be alone, Calum."

"That's not what I'm afraid of. How will I survive losing him if I let him in even more than I already have? Everything was easier when I was on my own."

"I think you know that's not true. You already love him. Keeping him at arm's length isn't going to change your feelings. The only thing it's doing is making you both miserable, and that's not a way to live, especially not when you love each other. I understand the fear. It's not exactly the same, but when Kari started going around the forest by himself, I was terrified. I'd been in hiding for most of my life, and it had always been just him and me. I thought for sure something would happen to him, and it did."

"So you were right not to want him to go?" Because that was what it sounded like.

But Julian shook his head. "What happened to him was good. He met Calder, and they fell in love. That wouldn't have happened if I'd insisted on keeping him with me, and I wouldn't know his son if I'd pushed him away."

"You couldn't push him away. He's your son."

"Maybe I couldn't, but I could have tried my best not to love him. I could have told him not to come back. I would still have worried, though, just like you'll still worry even if you tell Duane you can't be together. Besides, you're afraid of losing him, but if you let your fear win, you'll lose him anyway. If you want to be with him, you're going to have to get over it and understand that fear is a part of life. You can decide to obey it or ignore it as well as you can and live."

He was right. Calum was already losing Duane, and it was all because of his fear. He didn't think he'd ever be able to fully get over it, but being afraid didn't mean he couldn't live or be with Duane.

Things wouldn't be easy. They'd never been easy when it came to Calum's life, but in this case, he was complicating everything himself.

He had a choice. He could push everyone away, be alone for the rest of his life, and yearn for everything he could have had.

Or he could ignore the fear and live the life he'd never thought he could have but was just in front of him, waiting for him to make the right choice.

Duane held out a cup of coffee to Kaspar. Talia was cradled against Kaspar's chest, her eyes closed as she slept. She was a beautiful baby, but Duane thought all babies were beautiful. He didn't know many of them—or any beyond Cal and Talia, really—but the two of them were precious.

"Thank you," Kaspar said softly.

Duane filled a mug for himself, then hesitated. Since Calum had started keeping him at arm's length, he'd felt uncomfortable. Without Calum by his side, he wasn't sure this place was his home, and he felt like maybe he was intruding. He didn't think Julian and Kaspar would ask him to leave, but he'd started thinking that maybe he should.

Being so close to Calum hurt. He wished Calum had listened to him, and maybe he had. Maybe it was just that he couldn't deal with the fear, and Duane understood that. This wouldn't be the first relationship of his that ended because the person he was with couldn't take everything that came with his job.

But he'd really hoped things would be different with Calum.

"What's on your mind?" Kaspar asked.

Duane sighed and sat at the table in front of him. "Calum."

Kaspar nodded. "You have to understand what he's been through."

"I do understand. I don't blame him for freaking out after what happened or for being afraid. I just wish the fear wasn't stronger than the love he feels for me."

"I don't think it is. I just think he's not sure how to deal with it."

"Does anyone know how to deal with fear?"

"You do."

And it was something Duane had learned. Even then, he'd been terrified every time he was sent on a mission. Once he was working, though, it was fairly easy to ignore it.

But Calum's position was different. He was afraid something would happen to Duane like Duane was, but he didn't have anything to focus on. He had Julian, Kaspar, and the babies, but they couldn't be his entire life. Maybe finding a job would help him deal, or maybe it wouldn't. It hadn't helped in Duane's previous relationships.

But people in the military got married. They managed to find people who could deal with them being away and being afraid they wouldn't come back. Things should be easier for Calum since Duane wasn't going anywhere.

He sighed. "I'm just not sure what to do," he confessed. "I don't want to give up on him, even though he's pushing me away again. I understand what he went through and that he's still terrified something will happen to me. I just don't want to push him in a direction he doesn't want."

"He does want you."

"I'm aware of that. It might not be enough for him to want to deal with all of this, though. It's not for everyone."

Kaspar stared for a moment before nodding. "You've already been through this before."

"I had other relationships. None of them survived. I thought things would be easier with this new job, but clearly, I was wrong."

"Maybe not. But you didn't choose the easiest person to do this with."

"Yet I'd choose him again. I'm in love with him." But

sometimes, love wasn't enough. "Maybe I should move out. I was only supposed to be here to protect Calum, but we can find someone else." Foley was still out there, possibly plotting a way to get back to Calum. Thomas had talked to him and his council member, and things had calmed down, which was good, because with the shooting, they had other things to focus on.

"Do you *want* to move out?" Kaspar asked.

Talia hiccupped and started waking up, but Kaspar gently patted her back and shushed her back to sleep. Duane was mesmerized. He couldn't see himself in Kaspar's position, but he loved the two babies as if they were his. He could imagine a life in which he and Calum were the cool uncles, then went back home to their own house.

Would they have a chance at that?

He could only be honest. "I don't want to be away from Calum, or from you and Julian and the babies. I feel like this is my home."

"That's because it is. You're part of the family now. Eventually, you'll need your own space, but for now, we're happy to have you with us. Julian and I talked when we realized something was happening between you and Calum, and we agreed on that. We also agreed that you shouldn't give up."

Duane cocked his head. There was something in the way Kaspar was looking at him that told him he and Julian had decided they should intervene. "Has Julian decided to talk to Calum?"

Kaspar chuckled. "Right in one. He's the closest to Calum and the one who knows him best. If there's anyone who can make Calum see that what he's doing isn't going to help him or you, it's Julian. Have faith in him. Give Calum the chance to wrap his mind around what being with you means. He'll come to you."

Duane hoped so. He didn't want to lose Calum, but he also

didn't want to push Calum into something he didn't want. Maybe being with Duane would be too much for him. Duane wouldn't blame him for that, and he wouldn't be angry.

But he *would* be devastated.

He wanted Calum in his life. Hell, Calum *was* his life, or at least part of it. Duane didn't feel complete when Calum wasn't with him, and he wanted what they'd had before back.

But the decision was in Calum's hands. He already knew how Duane felt about him and what he wanted. There was nothing more Duane could do or say. He'd talked to Calum and had tried reassuring him, but there was no way to know if it would be enough.

Duane prayed it would be.

CHAPTER FOURTEEN

When Calum's phone rang and he saw Thomas's name on the screen, dread filled him. Lately, it had never been good when the alpha called him. Calum still had to answer, though, so he did.

"Hello?"

"Calum. How are you doing?" Thomas asked.

"Tired." And annoyed with himself.

He still hadn't talked to Duane, even though he meant to. There was just so much to do between Duane's job and the babies that he hadn't had the opportunity. He missed Duane, though. He wanted back what they'd had before, and he didn't want Duane to think things were over between them.

Thomas chuckled. "I can imagine, with two babies in the house. Do you think you can take a break? I need to talk to you."

"Am I going to regret coming over?"

Thomas laughed. "I'll make it better by offering you some pecan cookies my wife baked."

That perked Calum up. He loved cookies in all shapes and forms and almost every taste. "Done. When do you need to see me?"

"I'll be in my office for the rest of the afternoon, so come whenever you can."

Whenever he could had ended up being several hours later. He'd been on his way out when Talia had started crying, and since Kaspar was napping and Julian was in the bathroom, Calum had stepped in. He'd fed her, but she'd thrown up all over him, so he'd had to change. Once he'd done that, Cal had woken up, too, so Calum had handed Talia to Julian and grabbed the boy to take him to Kaspar. Then he'd realized he hadn't gotten anything ready for dinner yet, and he didn't know how long he'd be with Thomas, so he quickly put something together. It was only sandwiches, but he didn't have the energy to do more, and he hoped no one would mind. Duane probably wanted something more substantial after work, but Calum hoped he'd have time to work on that when he came back.

As much as he loved the babies and Julian and Kaspar, it felt good to be out of the house for a bit. Once he was far enough away that he wouldn't be able to hear the babies cry, Calum paused, closed his eyes, and took a deep breath.

He was slightly worried about whatever Thomas wanted to tell him, but he told himself not to be. Whatever it was, he wouldn't be alone facing it. It was something that had taken him a while to understand, but now, he did. Whatever happened, Kaspar and Julian would always support him. Duane might, too, if Calum could find the time to talk to him. He didn't know where they stood, but he promised himself that he'd find the time, even if he didn't have it.

Calum felt better when he reached Thomas's house and even more so when the alpha greeted him with a smile. Surely, it meant there was nothing wrong.

"I'm listening," he said as he settled back into a chair and stuffed half a cookie into his mouth.

Thomas looked amused, but his expression quickly shifted into something more serious. "With everything that happened with Jasper, it took me a while to get around to Foley."

The cookie suddenly tasted like ashes, and Calum quickly swallowed it. "What about him?"

"I told you I'd contact him. It's not even because of you, but because he came into our territory when he'd been warned he wasn't welcome. I had words for him, and I made sure he heard every single one of them. I also asked more questions and found out about the man you were supposed to marry."

Calum's mouth was dry. "Who is he?"

"A skunk shifter. Not the beta, but close enough to the alpha that he hoped that marrying a carrier would help him get some power. I've only given Jasper the bare bones considering he was shot only days ago, but he'll look into it."

"And Foley?"

"I told him that you're my problem now, not his. He knows to stay away from you, and if he doesn't, the bats will be in trouble. I have the weight of the council behind me, and he doesn't. I doubt he'll want to test me."

Thomas looked fierce, and Calum wouldn't want to test him, either. Foley had never been a bad man, but he also had never been a strong one. Hopefully, he'd stay away from Calum. He wouldn't like what happened to him if he didn't.

"So I don't want you to worry about any of this anymore," Thomas continued. "I'll talk to Duane. Tell him he doesn't need to stick around. I know the two of you are working things out, but I'm sure you'll both enjoy your freedom."

"Our freedom?" What was Thomas talking about?

"He just arrived in the forest. He didn't expect to have to share a house with three adult men and two babies, so he might be happy to be able to go back to the house he shared with the other guards. Besides, it won't be for long. I already selected several houses he might be interested in, and as soon as he selects one, we can start renovations."

The cookies Calum had eaten wanted to make a reappearance, but he swallowed and prayed it wouldn't happen.

Was Duane moving out? It certainly sounded like it, and Calum didn't know how to deal with it. This wasn't what he'd wanted when he'd freaked out about Duane getting hurt. This wasn't what he wanted, ever. He'd finally made his mind up and decided to talk to Duane, and now he was losing him? It wasn't fair. And why hadn't Duane talked to him about this? Why was he doing it behind his back?

"Calum?"

Thomas sounded worried, so Calum forced himself to smile. "I'm fine. Thank you for everything you did with Foley. I was starting to wonder if he'd ever leave me alone. I'm relieved to find out he will."

"I am, too. Keep an eye open for a while, just in case, but I don't think he'll be a problem again, at least not to you."

Calum wondered about Thomas's words, but he couldn't worry about other carriers that might be born in the colony. He didn't have the strength to do that, especially not now that he'd found out Duane was moving out.

Calum left Thomas's house. He felt like he was in a dream, unable to fully wrap his mind around what had happened. He was glad Foley would leave him alone, but what about Duane? How was Calum supposed to live without him?

Julian had been right. Losing Duane hurt, which meant it was too late and that Calum was in too deep. Even now that Duane was going back home and leaving Calum behind, Calum would worry about him. It would be even worse because he wouldn't see Duane every evening and reassure himself that Duane was all right.

Calum thought about all of that as he walked back home, knowing he needed to call Duane and ask him what was happening. He realized he wouldn't have to when he found Duane in front of the house, climbing the porch steps. He rushed forward, needing to talk to him, but stumbled on a root. He fell to his hands and knees, and tears prickled his eyes.

He was a disaster, but he was *Duane's* disaster. He never wanted that to change.

"Calum?" Duane called out.

Calum got back to his feet and brushed the snow off his hands and knees. He heard Duane come closer, and he didn't look up until he was done. He was afraid of how he'd react with Duane in front of him, and it was easier to speak without looking Duane in the eyes.

"Why are you moving out?" he asked.

"Moving out?" Duane asked.

He was in front of Calum now, so close yet so far.

"I thought you were in love with me. I thought you wanted to be with me and that you liked what we had. I don't want you to leave. I know I haven't been great lately, but I was scared of losing you, and I still am. But even if I lose you now, it won't change how much I hurt over it. I'm in love with you, and the thought of you moving out and leaving me behind hurts so badly that I almost wish I hadn't fallen for you."

Calum didn't want to beg, but it was a close thing. He'd been working so hard to create a new life for himself, and Duane was part of that life. Calum would survive if Duane left him, but he didn't know in what state, and he didn't want to find out.

Duane was confused. What was Calum talking about? Who had told him he was moving out?

Well, he might eventually, but not before his own place was ready. When that happened, he hoped Calum would move with him, but they hadn't talked about it, mostly because Duane had been afraid to push too hard. He'd known Calum was dealing with things at his own pace, and, especially after talking to Kaspar, he'd been reassured that things would be okay eventually.

But not if they were kicking him out.

Calum finally looked at him. His eyes were filling with

tears, and Duane didn't want him to cry, especially because he didn't understand what Calum was crying over. He opened his arms, unsure if Calum would take the offer, but thankfully, he did.

Calum made a strangled sound and threw himself into Duane's arms. Duane wrapped himself around him, holding him close and trying to understand what was happening.

"Tell me what's going on," he said. That was the only way he'd get the entire story.

"Thomas called me. He wanted to see me to let me know that Foley had been dealt with and that he'd found out who the man I was supposed to marry was. He's a skunk, and even though Jasper is wounded, he said he'd take care of it and talk to the guy. I don't have to marry anyone I don't want to marry, and I don't have to leave the cete."

"That's good."

"And Thomas said that since Foley seems to have understood he had to leave me alone after Thomas threatened him with the council, you could go back home. You don't have to stay with us anymore. I'm not in danger, and you moved here with us to protect me."

Duane was starting to understand where Calum's belief that he was moving out came from. "Did Thomas tell you I was moving out, or did you assume I would?"

Calum tensed. Duane didn't want him to think he was berating him, so he stroked a hand up and down Calum's back.

"I don't remember," Calum said in a tiny voice. "And Thomas did say he knew there was something between us. But he also said you'd be happy to go back home to your room, and maybe you will be. Living with two babies can't be easy when you have to work every day. It's a lot of work and noise, and if you want to move out, that's okay. It doesn't mean we have to break up, right?"

Calum had assumed a whole lot of things, but Duane

didn't blame him. They should have talked about this long ago, when they'd first realized they were falling in love. Maybe talking would have made things easier, or maybe not. There was no way to know, but now that they were in this situation, they needed to find a way out.

"I'm not going anywhere," Duane promised.

"Even if you move out?"

There was so much restrained hope in Calum's voice that it broke Duane's heart. No matter what Calum said, his life hadn't been easy. It didn't matter if he hadn't been physically abused like the other carriers. He'd still been hurt, and that pain had left scars.

"I'm not moving out," Duane told him. "As long as you don't want me to and Kaspar and Julian are okay with it, I'm staying with you."

"Are you sure? Because I know things haven't been easy lately. It was my fault, and I want things to get better, but I don't want to force you to stay if you don't want to."

Duane was aware of the fact that Calum found it easier to talk to him when he wasn't looking at him, but for this, Duane wanted to see him. He cupped the back of Calum's head and gently tilted it until they were looking at each other. Calum's gaze still jumped away from Duane every so often, but that was okay.

"I should have talked to you a while ago. I thought you needed time, and I didn't want to make things harder for you when you were already dealing with so much. Especially after the shooting, I thought you'd need time to wrap your mind around how you felt for me and what that meant for you. But I talked to Kaspar, and he confirmed that he and Julian want me to stay. If you want the same, then I don't see a reason for me to move out, at least not until my house is ready."

"Thomas said he'd made a list and that you could go and choose one."

That was the next step in Duane's life, and it was exciting. It felt even better knowing that he'd have Calum with him. "Then we should go and see this list."

"You want me to go with you?"

"I hope that eventually that house will be yours, too. I want you to like it and to be able to imagine yourself living in it with me. That will only happen if we choose it together, so yes, I'd like it if you came with me. You don't have to if you think this is too fast for you, though."

The tears finally dropped from Calum's eyes as he shook his head. Duane wasn't sure what was happening, but when Calum kissed him, he knew everything would be all right.

It didn't mean things wouldn't be hard. Duane had never been in a long-term relationship that actually lasted, and Calum was dealing with a lot, from his old alpha to his ex-boyfriend. It made sense that he was terrified to lose Duane, but it was something he'd have to learn to deal with. Duane would be there to help him through it, but there were some things that only Calum could work on.

But he'd always have Duane's support. Duane wasn't going anywhere, and eventually, the two of them would move in together and build a life. What that life meant or included didn't matter right now. The only thing that did was that they were together.

"Thank you," Calum whispered.

Duane kissed his forehead. "You have nothing to thank me for. I should have been more open with you, even though I was trying to give you space. I think that in certain situations, it might have been too much space for you. It gave you too much time to overthink things, and I could have helped put a stop to that."

Calum sighed. "You're probably right. I have no idea what I'm doing when it comes to relationships."

"You're not the only one. I'm pretty sure things will be

easier if we agree to talk to each other. When either of us has a problem or feels unhappy, that's what we should do. I don't want you to retreat into yourself like you did this time around. I can't help you when you do that."

"I'll talk to you next time," Calum promised. "As long as you're not bothered by me freaking out."

"I don't see how I could be. Everyone is afraid of something, and your fear is to lose me. It mirrors mine. I'll do anything I can to make sure I don't lose you."

"Never," Calum promised.

"The same goes for me. Unless you kick me out, I'm not going anywhere, and I'm never leaving you."

Calum pushed up and kissed Duane again. Duane cradled him to his chest, his heart still racing. He didn't know if he'd almost lost Calum, but it had been too close for him to be comfortable. But they'd talked and promised they'd both try their hardest to keep it. Their future was looking bright and clear.

EPILOGUE

Calum had been smiling for what felt like days. Maybe he had been, but who would blame him? When he'd arrived in badger territory, he'd been terrified and alone. Part of that was his fault, but he'd seen the light, and now, his future looked bright.

He had a loving boyfriend. Duane had never been more attentive than he was since they talked about him moving out, and while Calum felt a bit guilty, he also felt cherished in a way he'd never been before. Duane made him feel he was the center of his world, and Calum quite liked that.

He liked everything about his life. He was finally free, with Foley having retreated into bat territory. Calum barely left the cete, but he didn't want to. He was more than happy to stick around, be with his family, make friends with the other carriers, and just live.

He hadn't realized he already had all these things until recently. He'd been so afraid to lose everything that he hadn't realized how many things he had now. Many people would have felt it wasn't enough for them to help with the babies, but Calum loved it.

But not enough to have his own children. He might change his mind in time, but he didn't think he would. He loved Talia and Cal, but he didn't feel he was made to be a father. He was fine with being an uncle, and watching the babies grow up almost day by day was incredible.

The sound of someone crying made him smile. Life was never boring in a house with two newborns.

Everyone was downstairs except for Duane, who was at work. The babies had been asleep, but clearly, it was time for someone to eat. Since Kaspar and Julian were with the children in the living room, Calum wasn't worried about needing to make a bottle, but he grabbed two bottles of water from the fridge and headed to the living room.

Kaspar and Julian looked up when they heard him. Julian was cradling Talia to his chest, a sure sign she was the one who'd woken up. Cal seemed to still be asleep in the crib in the corner, but Calum still peeked on him as he walked by.

"Here," he said, giving Kaspar one of the bottles before leaving the second one on the table by the armchair where Julian was sitting.

Kaspar was curled up on the couch, most of his body buried under a blanket. He took the bottle with a thank you, and Calum sat next to him. He looked around, his heart feeling too full. These people were his family, and they loved him.

"I wanted to thank both of you," he said.

Kaspar frowned. "Why? What did we do?"

"What *didn't* you do? You could have said no when I asked to move in with the two of you so I could help with the babies. You barely knew me then, and I wouldn't have blamed you. Instead, you took me with you and gave me a home and family. I can never thank you enough for everything the two of you did."

"There's nothing to thank us for," Julian said. "We did what was right, and I'm glad. I got a second son out of it, and I never thought I could have that." His gaze drifted to Talia. "Just like I never thought I could have more children. I might not have had a hand in creating you, but it doesn't make you any less my son."

Calum hadn't come here to cry, yet his eyes prickled. Thankfully, they were happy tears this time, and he didn't have a problem rubbing his eyes and showing Julian and

Kaspar he was overwhelmed. "My parents weren't bad people, but they also weren't good parents. I think it was easier for them to keep their distance between us, especially after they realized I was a carrier. They knew I'd be taken from them sooner rather than later. I guess they did what I tried doing with Duane. They pushed me away so it wouldn't hurt as much when I was taken away from them."

"Do you think it worked for them? That they didn't feel as much pain when you came here?"

"I don't know."

What Calum did know was that even if his parents had been hurt by losing him, it was too late to fix things between them. Maybe if they'd explained what they were doing, Calum would have understood. He kind of did, even now. He just didn't think they could fix their relationship.

Besides, he didn't want to. He had no intention of ever setting foot in bat territory again. He was home with the cete and didn't need anything or anyone else.

"But I do know it wouldn't have worked for me," Calum continued. "I thought I'd lost Duane, and it hurt so much it felt like my heart was being torn out."

"I'm glad the two of you finally talked and fixed things," Kaspar said. "Although maybe next time, don't wait until things go that badly. I don't want you doing anything to get hurt over something that could be fixed as easily as having a conversation."

"I can't promise I won't ever be an idiot again, but I'll try not to be. When we talked, we agreed we'd have to talk to each other if we had a problem, and I think it was a good idea." It wouldn't work miracles, but at least he and Duane would know where the other stood.

Kaspar straightened and wrapped an arm around Calum's shoulders. He pulled him close for a sideways hug, and Calum was happy to go.

He'd never been a touchy-feely kind of person. He still wasn't, and if it had been anyone who wasn't part of his family doing this, he'd have been uncomfortable.

But he wasn't, because Kaspar was part of his family. Where Julian was a father figure, Kaspar felt like a big brother. Calum never had those two things, and he almost couldn't believe he finally did at twenty-one years old.

"We're happy for you," Julian said.

More importantly, Calum was happy for himself. He was allowing himself to be happy, which was much easier than trying to push everyone away for fear of being hurt. He had no doubt that eventually, he'd be hurt by someone or by something, but he'd deal with it when it happened.

In the meantime, he'd enjoy his life and make the most out of it.

Duane stared at the hole in the fence. It was big enough to let an adult through, and Duane had no doubt that was what happened. The only problem was that he didn't know if someone had come in or gone out.

Either was possible, which was worrying. If a shifter had snuck out of the forest, they'd be in danger, but there was little Duane could do about that. If someone had snuck in, though, the entire forest was in danger, and it was incredibly frustrating that even then, there was nothing Duane could do. How was he supposed to find one person in the entire forest? They didn't even know who they were looking for—if they were a man or a woman, what they looked like, or anything else.

A noise behind him made him turn. When he and Saul had found the hole, he'd sent Saul to get Thomas. The alpha needed to see this, but Duane had no idea what he'd do to fix it. Was there even a way to fix what happened? They could close the hole in the fence, and they'd no doubt do it, but what about the person who'd come in?

Because Duane had no doubt that was what happened. Some shifters probably wanted out of the forest, and some might have even escaped over the years, but considering what was happening just outside their gate, it would be foolish to sneak out now. There were humans everywhere on the other side of the fence, walking around as if their presence was the only reason shifters were locked in. If someone had gone out, they'd have been found.

"What happened?" Thomas asked when he reached Duane.

Duane stepped aside to give Thomas space to see the hole. "We found it like this."

"In or out?" Thomas crouched next to the hole and prodded at what was left of the fence.

"I'm pretty sure someone came in. It could be either way, but see how the fence is folded here and here?" Duane asked as he pointed out what he'd noticed. "It looks like someone pushed in from the outside."

Thomas nodded. "I agree. Besides, most shifters wouldn't have had a problem climbing the fence. The same can't be said for humans."

And if a shifter had tried sneaking out, it would have been a badger, at least in this area of the forest. Thomas would know if someone was missing. "So we have a human in the forest." Thomas got to his feet. "One who doesn't belong."

"How are we going to find them?" Saul asked.

The three of them looked at each other. Duane didn't have any idea how they could do this or even if it was possible. It would be hard for a human to hide in one of the territories, but if they managed to get to Northwood or even one of the smaller towns, they could. They had to be on foot, which would make it more dangerous, but they wouldn't have snuck in without a plan. That meant they knew what they were doing and probably where they were going.

Thomas rubbed his face. "This is the last thing we needed."

Duane agreed. "You think it's related to the shootings?" He still wasn't convinced humans weren't involved. The shooter had to have been a shifter, but it didn't mean they weren't working with someone outside the forest. Maybe that someone had finally decided to step in.

"Maybe someone is trying to make it look like humans are involved. It would be easier to blame humans we don't know and who we can't trust than a shifter who's lived here most of their life."

"Even considering what some of the shifter groups have done?"

"Some people in the forest are awful, and the horrors I've seen mean I don't trust them. I know shifters, though. We fight each other, but we'd never let the humans take over."

"Someone might have."

"You're right. I don't know every single shifter in the forest, and I have no doubt that some of them want out. I don't know what they're trying to do with this, but it can't be good. I already asked someone to come around and see if they can find a trail. The problem is that we don't know when that hole was made. Besides, the snow won't make it any easier."

"But there's no other way to find whoever this was," Duane murmured.

"Unfortunately, I don't think so. It snowed, so we can't see anything on the ground, and they could have gone anywhere from here. They didn't reach the center of the cete where the houses are, which is good, but there's no way to know which way they went if we can't find a trail. Our territory borders with the bears, the foxes, the bobcats, and the rodents. I doubt whoever this was went toward the rodents. I have full trust in the bears and the bobcats, but it doesn't mean this person isn't hiding in their territory. Besides, Northwood is right there. It would be easy to hide out once they reached it."

And impossible to find them.

Thomas sighed. "Why don't the two of you go home? There's nothing more you can do here, and it's starting to snow again. Get some rest, because I think that whatever will happen next, it won't be easy."

Unfortunately, Duane agreed. Someone wanted to hurt the shifters in the forest, and there was no way to find out who it was. There were plenty of humans out there who had it in for shifters and didn't want them to have equal rights or be set free. Duane understood the fear, but it didn't warrant whatever these people were doing.

He and Saul trudged in the snow toward the center of the cete as soon as Thomas was joined by several badgers who worked cete security. Duane wished there was more he could do, but he wouldn't know where to start. The only thing was to wait and see what happened.

And pray no one would get hurt in the meantime.

When Calum heard the front door open, he smiled and nearly bounced on his feet.

Duane was home.

It was early, but Calum wasn't going to argue. The more time he spent with Duane, the happier he was. He turned to face his boyfriend as he walked into the kitchen, but the smile on his lips froze.

Something had happened. Calum didn't need to ask to know. Duane's expression was enough to tell him that Duane was worried about something, even though when Duane looked up and saw Calum, he smiled.

Duane wrapped an arm around Calum's waist, pulled him closer to kiss his temple, and buried his face against Calum's hair. "How was your day?" he asked.

"The usual. Your day didn't go as well, though."

"How do you know?"

"Your expression. Something happened, right?" Calum was almost afraid to ask.

Duane sighed and stepped away. He rubbed his hands on his face, looking more tired than he had in a long time. "Don't tell anyone you don't trust about this, but we found a hole in the fence. Someone came in, but we have no idea who or why. The only thing we know is that it can't be good."

A chill of fear climbed up Calum's spine. "There's a human in the forest?"

"A human who shouldn't be here, yes. That's what we think, anyway, although Thomas will have more information once whoever he chooses to sniff around the hole does their job. He was hoping they'd find a trail, but I doubt they'll be able to with the snow."

"Do we have to worry?" Were they safe in the house? What about the babies?

"I think we should be careful. But I can't think of one reason whoever came in would have to come around here. They're here for a reason, and it's not to break into houses. Besides, I'm pretty sure Thomas will reinforce security. With me here, you don't have to worry about anything."

Calum wanted to believe him, but how could he? And what about when Duane went to work?

Duane wrapped an arm around his shoulders and pulled him closer. "Hey, I don't want you to worry. I know this is scary and that me telling you everything will be okay doesn't mean you believe me. But many people around here are ready to protect you and your family. Thomas will make sure that whoever came in isn't in badger territory anymore, and I'm sure that once Luther and his people find out about this, they'll do everything they can, too. Humans have cameras on their side of the fence to ensure no shifter tries sneaking out, so they might have caught something. I know this is scary, but please, don't allow fear to take over."

Calum sucked in a breath. Duane was right. He'd let fear guide his steps until now, and it hadn't worked out. He needed to let go of all of this and trust Duane, Thomas, and everyone else.

"We'll be fine," Calum said.

Duane smiled. "We will. It's good to see that you're convinced of it, though. I was afraid you'd freak out again."

Calum almost had, but he was done with all of that. Fear had almost taken Duane away from him, and he wouldn't allow it to happen, not now, not in the future. His life was nowhere near perfect, but it was perfect for him, and he wasn't giving it up without a fight. It didn't matter who or what he had to fight, either.

No matter how many storms they had to weather, he and Duane would do it together and stand strong until the skies cleared again.

ABOUT THE AUTHOR

Catherine is the creator of several series, most of them paranormal, including the Whitedell Pride Series and the Gillham Pack Series. While she graduated in translation, she decided to go the writer's way because it was more fun to create her own stories and characters.

She's been living in Italy for more than twenty years, but she's a daughter of the North — Belgium to be precise — and she misses it so much that she's already planning to move back.

She loves pizza — probably too much — her son, her pets, and of course, books. She sneaks some reading time into her schedule every time she has five minutes free from writing, demands from her various pets and son, and lastly, housework.

Connect with her:

lievens.catherine@gmail.com
BookBub: https://www.bookbub.com/authors/catherine-lievens
Website: https://authorcatherinelievens.com/
Facebook: https://www.facebook.com/catherine.lievens.9
Facebook Group: https://www.facebook.com/groups/411788002341528/
Twitter: https://twitter.com/authorCLievens
Newsletter: http://eepurl.com/c-uvKn